MAKING IT CONNECT
GOD'S STORY: GENESIS — REVELATION

MW01180660

SMALL GROUP LEADER'S GUIDEBOOK

Life application activities, discussion questions, community building helps

Jonah's Great Escape

BUNCH OF BABBLIN' BABYLONIANS BUILD BIG BUILDING

STORY ON PAGE 2

News... get your news here!

LOOK!

A giant gift!

WILLOW CREEK RESOURCES

ZONDERVAN™

grades 2/3

SMALL GROUP LEADER'S GUIDEBOOK
MAKING IT CONNECT
God's Story: Genesis – Revelation

Copyright © 2000 Willow Creek Community Church

Requests for information should be addressed to:
Willow Creek Association
P.O. Box 3188
Barrington, IL 60011-3188

Executive Director of Promiseland: Sue Miller

Creative Team: Deanna Armentrout, Pat Cimo, Graeme Franks, Dave Huber, Marta Johnson, Kevin Koesterer, Holly Laurent, Sandra McFarland, Sue Miller, Dean Peterson, Susan Shadid

Editorial Team: Jorie Dahlin, Janet Quinn, Nancy Raney

Designer: Barsuhn Design Incorporated
Cover Illustrator: Laurie Keller
Interior Illustrator: Mary Lynn Blasutta

Many thanks to: the Promiseland staff team as a whole who continually contribute, our volunteers who help put supplies together each weekend, and the volunteers who try out, test, and evaluate this curriculum to give us feedback along the way.

All Scripture quotations, unless otherwise indicated, are taken from the Holy Bible: New International Version®. Copyright © 1973, 1978, 1984 by International Bible Society. Used by permission of Zondervan Publishing House. All rights reserved.

All rights reserved. No part of this publication may be reproduced, stored in a retrieval system, or transmitted in any form or by any means—electronic, mechanical, photocopy, recording, or any other—except for brief quotations in printed reviews or otherwise noted, without prior permission of the Willow Creek Association.

Printed in the United States of America.

WILLOW CREEK RESOURCES   ZONDERVAN™

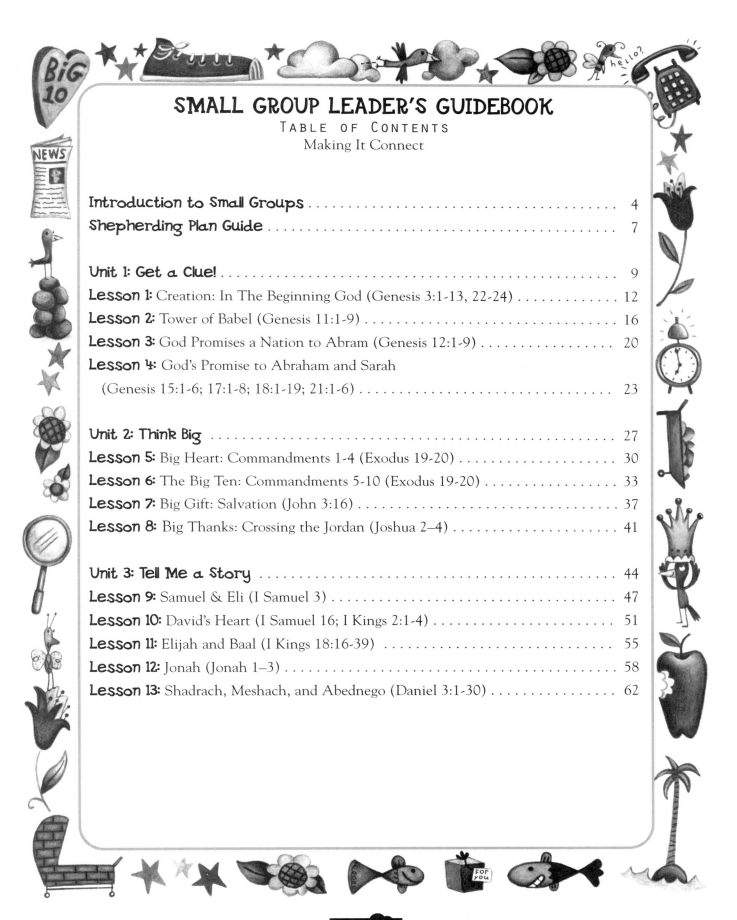

SMALL GROUP LEADER'S GUIDEBOOK
TABLE OF CONTENTS
Making It Connect

© 2000 Willow Creek Community Church / Small Group Leader's Guidebook

Introduction to Small Groups

Why Have Small Groups?

Developing a children's ministry in which children are known and cared for and through which children's hearts are touched and changed means creating a ministry in which relationships can be built. Life change happens best within the context of relationships and Small Groups can serve as the structure for relationships to develop and grow.

Who Leads a Small Group?

The ministry model for using the Promiseland Curriculum includes a structured Small Group Time. This time, during which 8-10 kids and one shepherd/leader meet together, is the key time for relationships and community to be built and for children to begin to see the relevant application of the Bible truth to everyday life. Because the main goal of Small Groups is to build relationships and intentionally shepherd the children, the leader of the Small Group is someone who has the spiritual gift of shepherding and is

called a Shepherd. Below is a chart showing the difference between a Shepherd and a Teacher.

The following characteristics have been identified as those of effective Shepherds of children.

1. They see their role as a facilitator to apply the curriculum. They take the curriculum and put it into action.
2. They create an environment in which relationships can develop.
   - The environment is physically and emotionally safe.
   - They speak to the children in respectful ways.
   - They ask the children questions.
   - They maintain strong eye contact.
   - They listen carefully.
   - They use appropriate touch.
   - They are on time to greet the children.
   - They arrive prepared.
   - They are on eye level with the children.

Teacher	Small Group Leader
• Teaches curriculum	• Curriculum is applied
• Children learn something	• Children relate to the leader
• Children associate the teachers as being with children's ministry	• Association is with a child's life, both in and outside of children's ministry
	• Lifetime friendships
	• Hearts are touched
	• Children feel cared for
	• Children long for more

© 2000 Willow Creek Community Church / Small Group Leader's Guidebook

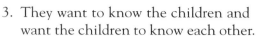

3. They want to know the children and want the children to know each other.

4. They provide focused attention with the children during Activity Stations, Kid Connection, Small Group Time, and time outside of the ministry within stated guidelines.

5. They have a desire to help children develop spiritually, to become more Christlike. They model an authentic walk in front of the kids.
   - They share their own personal spiritual development.
   - They pray for their children.
   - They model Christlikeness.

6. They encourage children verbally, with body language, and with written notes or cards.

7. They connect with the child's parents.
   - They introduce themselves to the parents.
   - They inquire about the rest of the family.
   - They inform them about their child in Promiseland.
   - They invite them to be a part of Promiseland.

How Do Small Groups Fit Into the Lesson?

There are two times during the lesson in which Small Groups meet together. The first time is just prior to the Large Group Program. As children enter the room in which the Large Group Program will take place they find their Small Group Leader and sit together as a group. They then participate in Kid Connection.

Kid Connection is a five-minute time for the group members to get to know each other. Questions are asked to encourage the children to share on a personal level. For example, "What is your idea of a perfect Saturday?" "If you could spend 15 minutes with any one person, who would it be?" Often the question is loosely tied to the key concept of the lesson. After the children have answered the question, the Small Group Leader lets the group know a little bit about what will happen in the Large Group Program and what to look for in the story.

The second time the Small Group meets together is after the Large Group Program. This is Small Group Time and is usually 20 minutes in length. This is the key time for intentional shepherding to occur and is designed to build community. The shepherd-leaders aid in the application of the teaching as well as minister to the kids personally. It is in the Small Group Time that each child becomes well known and receives encouragement. They are given an example of authentic Christianity as the leader shares his or her life with them, and children are helped to grow in their faith. During this time, children participate in fun learning activities that make the Bible lessons relevant to their lives. The NOW WHAT? objective is addressed during the Small Group Time. Through application-oriented games, conversation, and prayer with their Small Group Leader, kids explore ways to live out the biblical truths taught during the Large Group Program.

© 2000 Willow Creek Community Church / Small Group Leader's Guidebook

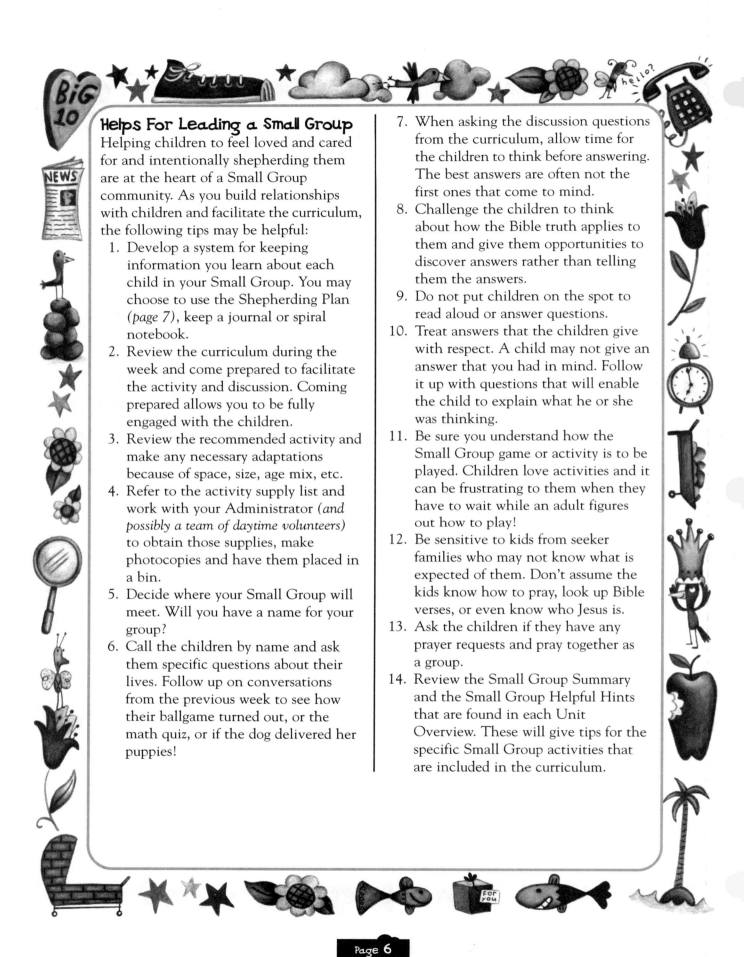

Helps For Leading a Small Group

Helping children to feel loved and cared for and intentionally shepherding them are at the heart of a Small Group community. As you build relationships with children and facilitate the curriculum, the following tips may be helpful:

1. Develop a system for keeping information you learn about each child in your Small Group. You may choose to use the Shepherding Plan (*page 7*), keep a journal or spiral notebook.

2. Review the curriculum during the week and come prepared to facilitate the activity and discussion. Coming prepared allows you to be fully engaged with the children.

3. Review the recommended activity and make any necessary adaptations because of space, size, age mix, etc.

4. Refer to the activity supply list and work with your Administrator (*and possibly a team of daytime volunteers*) to obtain those supplies, make photocopies and have them placed in a bin.

5. Decide where your Small Group will meet. Will you have a name for your group?

6. Call the children by name and ask them specific questions about their lives. Follow up on conversations from the previous week to see how their ballgame turned out, or the math quiz, or if the dog delivered her puppies!

7. When asking the discussion questions from the curriculum, allow time for the children to think before answering. The best answers are often not the first ones that come to mind.

8. Challenge the children to think about how the Bible truth applies to them and give them opportunities to discover answers rather than telling them the answers.

9. Do not put children on the spot to read aloud or answer questions.

10. Treat answers that the children give with respect. A child may not give an answer that you had in mind. Follow it up with questions that will enable the child to explain what he or she was thinking.

11. Be sure you understand how the Small Group game or activity is to be played. Children love activities and it can be frustrating to them when they have to wait while an adult figures out how to play!

12. Be sensitive to kids from seeker families who may not know what is expected of them. Don't assume the kids know how to pray, look up Bible verses, or even know who Jesus is.

13. Ask the children if they have any prayer requests and pray together as a group.

14. Review the Small Group Summary and the Small Group Helpful Hints that are found in each Unit Overview. These will give tips for the specific Small Group activities that are included in the curriculum.

© 2000 Willow Creek Community Church / Small Group Leader's Guidebook

SHEPHERDING PLAN GUIDE

How Well Am I Building the Relationship?

Children are fearfully and wonderfully made. Each one is unique and special, designed and loved by God. Often times, the children do not know this truth. The chart below is a simple tool to help Shepherds know their sheep and can help the children believe they are God's wonderful creation. This chart is meant to help you, as a Small Group Leader, shepherd your Small Group.

Names of Group Members

Key Areas/What do I know?

FAMILY HISTORY	1	2	3	4	5	6	7	8	9	10
Family Information										
Spiritual Information										
KEY QUESTIONS: DO I KNOW ...										
How this child expresses love and how he or she needs love expressed to him/her?										
How this child learns best?										
What makes this child sad?										
What makes this child happy?										
What frightens this child?										
What this child likes to do?										
Who this child's heroes are? Why he or she picked them to be heroes?										
What people or characters are influential in the life of this child?										
What key interests this child has?										
CHURCH HISTORY										
How long has this child been in this children's ministry?										
Other church experiences?										
What is this child's favorite thing about coming to this children's ministry program?										
Has this child told his or her friends about this children's ministry?										

© 2000 Willow Creek Community Church / Small Group Leader's Guidebook

PRAYING FOR THE CHILDREN YOU SHEPHERD

The Bible has many examples of Jesus talking about children. Here are a few for you to use as an inspiration for your prayers.

Matthew 18:3
And He said: "I tell you the truth, unless you change and become like little children, you will never enter the kingdom of heaven."

My Prayer:

_____
_____
_____
_____
_____

Matthew 19:14
Jesus said, "Let the little children come to me, and do not hinder them, for the kingdom of heaven belongs to such as these."

My Prayer:

_____
_____
_____
_____
_____

Mark 9:37
"Whoever welcomes one of these little children in my name welcomes me; and whoever welcomes me does not welcome me but the one who sent me."

My Prayer:

_____
_____
_____
_____
_____

© 2000 Willow Creek Community Church / Small Group Leader's Guidebook

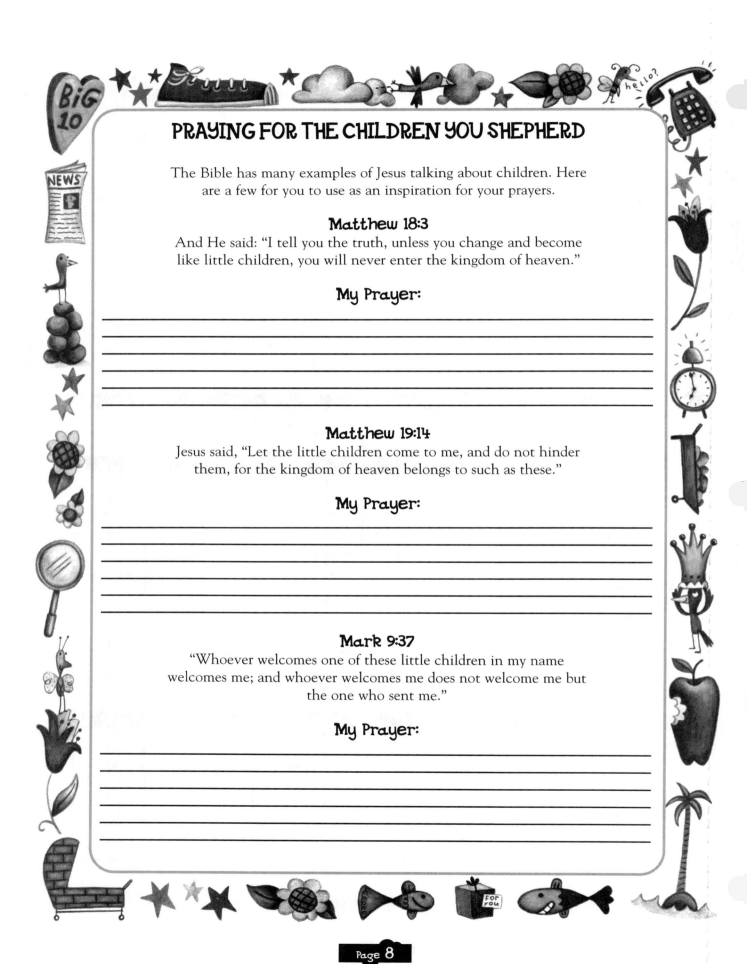

Get a Clue!
Unit 1 Overview

Unit Summary

This first unit of the new Promiseland year begins our sequential journey through the Bible. It looks at Creation and the First Families from some of the stories in Genesis and Exodus. This unit is set up as a mystery game. Each week, the kids will be solving mysteries in order to figure out the Bible stories and apply them to their lives.

Lesson Overviews

Lesson 1

Creation: In The Beginning God . . . (Genesis 3:1-13, 22-24)
Key Concept: God is holy and perfect and I need to obey Him.
Bible Verse: "This is love for God, to obey His commands.' 1 John 5:3
Know What: Children will learn how Adam and Eve committed the first sin when they disobeyed God in the garden.
So What: Children will be told God is holy and perfect.
Now What: Children will participate in an activity where they will discuss the consequences of choices and be challenged to obey.

Lesson 2

The Tower of Babel (Genesis 11:1-9)
Key Concept: God is #1 and we need to give Him all the credit.
Bible Verse: "For our Lord God Almighty reigns." Revelation 19:6
Know What: Children will hear the story of the Tower of Babel and how the Babylonians built a tower to their own greatness.
So What: Children will learn that God is #1 – He is sovereign.
Now What: Children will be challenged to give God the credit for everything they do.

Lesson 3

God Promises a Nation to Abram (Genesis 12:1-9)
Key Concept: God is good so I can trust Him and obey even when I don't understand.
Bible Verse: "He is good; His love endures forever." II Chronicles 5:13
Know What: Children will hear the story of Abram and Sarai. They will learn how Abram followed God and how God promised to bless him and make a great nation from his family.
So What: Children will learn God is good and He wants to bless us.
Now What: Children will be challenged to trust and obey God's commands even when they don't understand.

    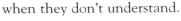  

© 2000 Willow Creek Community Church / Small Group Leader's Guidebook

Lesson 4

God's Promise to Abraham and Sarah (Genesis 15:1-6; 17:1-8; 18:1-19; 21:1-6)

Key Concept: God is a promise keeper so I can obey God and wait.

Bible Verse: "The Lord is faithful to all His promises." Psalm 145:13

Know What: Children will hear the story of Abraham and Sarah and how God promised them a son.

So What: Children will learn that God is a promise keeper.

Now What: Children will be challenged to trust and wait patiently for God to keep His promises to them.

Large Group Presentation Summary

The teaching method used in each of the four lessons of this first unit is a "Detective Solves Mystery" format. Each lesson is interactive as the teacher leads the children in discovering clues to figure out the Bible story. The first week the clues are found in boxes, the second week the clues are found in envelopes, the third week the clues are found in bags, and the fourth week the clues make up a word puzzle.

Large Group Helpful Hints

1. Each week during the Pre-Teach, the leader will discover detective gear to wear during the lesson. Take care to gather and then store the props carefully so that they are available each week. It will save you time and money!

2. Part of the fun of this lesson is the presentation of the clues and detective gear. Think of fun, creative ways to get these items to the leader during the Pre-Teach. A couple of ideas are to attach a pulley to the ceiling and drop them down, pull them across the stage with fishing wire, or put them on top of a remote control car. Or, you can have a prop assistant dressed as a detective, delivering clues and equipment.

3. Bags, boxes, and envelopes are used to hold clues. Make them as creative and colorful as possible. You can use brightly-colored gift bags, or use paint or colorful paper to make bags or boxes look interesting.

4. There is an element of repetition and review used throughout these lessons. This repetition will help kids remember the story and keep them involved in the lesson.

5. The lessons are enhanced by mysterious sounding music. You can find such tapes and CDs at a local music store or library.

6. These lessons are very interactive. Have fun with the kids. Get them involved. Using the "Get it! (Got it!) Good!" routine helps kids stay engaged in the lesson.

© 2000 Willow Creek Community Church / Small Group Leader's Guidebook

Small Group Summary

Small Group is the place where kids have the opportunity to actively begin to apply the Bible truth to their lives. For this unit, they are playing a game called, "Get A Clue!" The game packet is included in your curriculum kit. The game is played a little differently each week with the same gameboard. In week one, children will discuss the consequences of choices. In week two, they will consider giving God the credit for everything good. In week three, they will be challenged to trust and obey God even when they don't understand. In week four, they will look at promises God has made to His people.

Small Group Helpful Hints

1. Take good care of the game packets. Some pieces will be used more than once, so you will want to be sure they are in good condition.

2. The Situation and Location cards included in the game will be challenging for second and third grade children. They will need analytical thinking that may require help from a leader. Help the kids as they answer the questions.

3. If you have a few children who are uncomfortable reading aloud, step in and read for them.

4. During the game, don't show surprise or judgement by any of their answers. The purpose of this game is to explore their understanding of God's promises and His role in their lives today.

5. Try to keep the children's attention on the key concept of the lesson, not on winning the game.

6. Don't forget to make use of the Shepherding Plan Guide to get to know the children in your Small Group. As time allows, pray specifically for prayer requests raised by children in your Small Group.

© 2000 Willow Creek Community Church / Small Group Leader's Guidebook

Get a Clue!
Creation: In The Beginning God . . .

In the beginning when God made the whole earth and everything in it, God also created a beginning to His story. In these upcoming lessons, children will learn the many different eras of God's story within the Old Testament. They will learn about Creation, the first families, and God's promise of salvation. Children will then hear about the Exodus out of Egypt, the Conquests, God's different Kingdoms and the Exile of His people. Our hope within these lessons is to create a sequential view of the Old Testament to make a connection with how people and events fit together, as well as see how we can become part of God's story.

BIBLE STORY

Genesis 3:1-13, 22-24

Our first "Get a Clue" lesson reviews the account of creation as well as tells the story of Adam and Eve. Adam and Eve were the first man and woman whom God created and they committed the first sin when they disobeyed God. Because of their sin, Adam and Eve were separated from God because He is holy. They paid a consequence for choosing to disobey God.

KEY CONCEPT:
God is holy and perfect and I need to obey Him.

BIBLE VERSE

"This is love for God: to obey His commands." 1 John 5:3

OBJECTIVES

KNOW WHAT (LG): Children will learn how Adam and Eve committed the first sin when they disobeyed God in the garden.

SO WHAT (LG): Children will be told that God is holy and perfect.

NOW WHAT (SG): Children will participate in an activity where they will discuss the consequences of choices and be challenged to obey.

SPIRITUAL FORMATION

Obedience

IN ADVANCE DONE BY YOUR ADMINISTRATOR

• Photocopy the Character Cards, Mystery Card, and Location Cards onto colored cardstock for Week 1 from the Get a Clue! Game Packet. Cut out each card. Each group needs only ONE Mystery Card.

• Make Secret Envelopes by gathering seven plain envelopes per group. Write one of the following locations on each of the envelopes: Home, School, Theater, Mall, Restaurant, Sports, Park. Photocopy and cut out the Solution Cards/Try Again Cards and place one card inside each envelope.

• Gather different game pieces – one per child. Suggestions for game pieces: colored chips, colorful erasers, M&M® candies, etc.

• Place the above-mentioned cards along

© 2000 Willow Creek Community Church / Small Group Leader's Guidebook

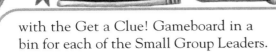

with the Get a Clue! Gameboard in a bin for each of the Small Group Leaders.

LEADER'S PREP

Most of life is made up of small choices. These choices can almost always be broken down into two categories. You're either going to follow and obey God or follow your own way and desires. It seems simple, but it's not. People have struggled with this choice from the very beginning. In preparation this week, please read the account of Adam and Eve in Genesis 3:1-24. As you read, look for the 'seemingly' small choices that lead to destruction. Then, this week watch and look for the small choices that you make. Intentionally try to determine the motivation behind your choices. (For encouragement read Psalm 1.)

KID CONNECTION (5 minutes)

WELCOME the children to Promiseland and share with them how glad you are they are in your group this year.

INTRODUCE yourself and have the children introduce themselves.

TELL the group, "What an exciting year we are going to have together. We will be doing and learning fun things, and it will be special to spend the year together as a group."

SHARE with the children one or two of your favorite things you did this summer.

ASK the children, "What was one of your favorite things from this summer?"

ASK the children, "Can you imagine what it would be like if we could put all of those great things together and make a perfect world?"

ENCOURAGE them to share what would make a perfect world.

TRANSITION

TELL the children, "All the things you just shared might have been what it was like when God first created the world! When God first created the world, it was totally perfect! Today in Large Group that's what we're going to hear about. We all know our world is not perfect now. Your mission during Large Group is to try and figure out when and what happened to make the world not perfect."

© 2000 Willow Creek Community Church / Small Group Leader's Guidebook

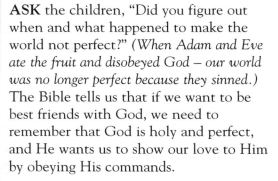

SMALL GROUP (20 minutes)

REVIEW

ASK the children, "Did you figure out when and what happened to make the world not perfect?" (*When Adam and Eve ate the fruit and disobeyed God – our world was no longer perfect because they sinned.*) The Bible tells us that if we want to be best friends with God, we need to remember that God is holy and perfect, and He wants us to show our love to Him by obeying His commands.

ACTIVITY: GET A CLUE! GAME SUPPLIES PROVIDED BY YOUR ADMINISTRATOR

- One Get a Clue! Gameboard
- Character Cards/Who, What, Where Cards - one per child (Week 1)
- Location Cards (Week 1)
- Secret Envelopes with a Solution Card or Try Again Card in each (Week 1)
- One Mystery Card (Week 1)
- Bible Verse Cards
- Pencils
- Game pieces

NOTES TO THE LEADER

The purpose of this game is to give children an opportunity in a non-threatening way to share their thoughts on specific situations requiring obedience to God. They will be challenged to identify the negative and positive consequences to choices.

- Be sensitive to the children who are not comfortable reading the game cards out loud by reading the cards for them.
- Read the Mystery Card to the children. As the children share their answers to the Location Cards, encourage them to discuss their reasons.
- Please reinforce that consequences are good when we obey.

SET UP

EXPLAIN to the children that the goal of the game is to get a clue from different locations on the board in order to solve the mystery.

PASS to each player a pencil and a game piece.

HAVE each player choose a Who, What, Where/Character Card. This is who they will be for the game.

OPEN up the gameboard and place it in the center of the group.

PLACE the Secret Envelopes around the outside of the game board, then place the Location Cards face down on top of the corresponding Secret Envelope.

TELL the children, "Inside each envelope will either be a clue to solve the mystery or a card that says, 'Try Again.'"

HAVE the players place their game pieces at a location of their choice on the gameboard.

INSTRUCTIONS

READ the Mystery Card.

PICK a player to start the game. Players start by answering the question on the Location Card that corresponds to the location on the gameboard that they picked.

AFTER answering the question, the child can be given the Secret Envelope from that location. If they get an envelope with a Solution Card, they need to write it down

© 2000 Willow Creek Community Church / Small Group Leader's Guidebook

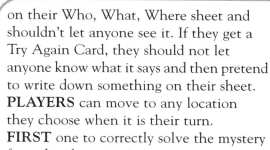

on their Who, What, Where sheet and shouldn't let anyone see it. If they get a Try Again Card, they should not let anyone know what it says and then pretend to write down something on their sheet.
PLAYERS can move to any location they choose when it is their turn.
FIRST one to correctly solve the mystery from the clues wins!
MYSTERY ANSWER: *Who:* Kid Tuesday; *What:* baseball cards *Where:* coat pockets

WRAP UP

TELL the children, "There are always consequences to sin. We don't always think about them, but there are! For every choice we make there is a consequence - sometimes it's really good and sometimes bad. Remember Adam and Eve? They made a choice to eat the fruit that God told them not to eat, and the consequence of their choice is that now we live in a world that is no longer perfect! You see, God is holy and perfect, and He wants every good thing for us. He knows that sin just messes things up! That's why He wants us to obey Him."

BIBLE VERSE

"This is love for God: to obey His commands." 1 John 5:3
REVIEW what this verse means.
REPEAT the verse with the children out loud.
GIVE each child a verse card and ask them to think about one way they will love God by obeying His commands this week.

PRAYER

Dear God,
We are glad that You are holy and perfect. Help us to show our love for You by obeying Your commands. Amen.

KID CONNECTION CONTINUES . . .

Small Group Leaders – This is a time for you and your group to: continue to build community, let your kids know you care about them and pray for them, hear their felt needs, and better equip you in knowing how to specifically reach out to each child. Here are questions that might help you:

ASK the children, "What are you looking forward to this next week? What are you not looking forward to this next week? Why?"

© 2000 Willow Creek Community Church / Small Group Leader's Guidebook

Get a Clue!
Tower of Babel

In the beginning when God made the whole earth and everything in it - God also created a beginning to His story. In these units kids will learn the many different eras of God's story within the Old Testament. They will learn about Creation, the first families, about God's promise of salvation. Children will then hear about the Exodus out of Egypt, the Conquests, God's different Kingdoms and the Exile of His people. Our hope within these lessons is to create a sequential view of the Old Testament to make it connect and show how people and events fit together – and to see how we can become part of God's story.

BIBLE STORY
Genesis 11:1-9
In this lesson children will hear the story of the Tower of Babel. Because of their pride, the Babylonians wanted to build a huge tower to show how great they were. God, however, ended the Babylonians' efforts by creating new languages so they wouldn't understand each other and by scattering them all over the earth. This story shows God's sovereignty and power. He is #1 and humanity is to humbly give Him the credit for all that is done.

KEY CONCEPT: God is #1 and we need to give Him all the credit.

BIBLE VERSE
"For our Lord God Almighty reigns." Revelation 19:6

OBJECTIVES
KNOW WHAT (LG): Children will hear the story of the Tower of Babel and how the Babylonians built a tower to their own greatness.
SO WHAT (LG): Children will learn that God is #1 – He is sovereign.
NOW WHAT (SG): Children will be challenged to give God the credit for everything they do.

SPIRITUAL FORMATION
Humility

IN ADVANCE DONE BY YOUR ADMINISTRATOR
• Photocopy the Who, What Where/Character Cards, Mystery Card, and Location Cards onto colored cardstock for Week 2 from the Get a Clue! Game Packet. Cut out each card. Each group needs only ONE Mystery Card.
• Make Secret Envelopes by gathering seven plain envelopes per group. Write one of the following locations on each of the envelopes: Home, School, Theater, Mall, Restaurant, Sports, Park. Photocopy and cut out the Solution Cards/Try Again Cards and place one card inside each envelope.
• Gather different game pieces – one per child. Suggestions for game pieces:

© 2000 Willow Creek Community Church / Small Group Leader's Guidebook

colored chips, colorful erasers, M&M® candies, etc.
• Place the above-mentioned cards along with the Get a Clue! Gameboard in a bin for each of the Small Group Leaders.

LEADER'S PREP

In our culture we use many things to show how great we are – or how smart – or educated – or wealthy – or spiritual. We use things like houses, cars, and maxed-out credit cards. We can easily run down a list of our accomplishments and accreditation showing our knowledge and experience. Now, none of these things are inherently bad. They only become dangerous when we fail to acknowledge where all the stuff, titles, and knowledge come from. When it becomes all about us and not about God, we choose to sin and be just like the Babylonians. This week read Genesis 11:1-9. Prayerfully consider the things in your life that make you feel great about yourself – or things that 'show' others something great you want them to know about you. In quiet moments this week, examine your heart and pray for ways you can give credit to God for what you have.

KID CONNECTION (5 minutes)

WELCOME the kids to Promiseland and share with them how glad you are that they are here.
INTRODUCE yourself to the kids.
HAVE the kids introduce themselves to each other.
ASK the kids, "Which one of the following describes what you are BEST at: Math, Science, or Reading?"
ASK the kids, "Which one of the following describes what you are BEST at: Painting, Writing, or Building?"
ASK the kids, "Which one of the following describes what you are BEST at: Sports or Music?"

TRANSITION

TELL the kids, "God made each of us to be great at different things! Maybe it's art or sports, or maybe it's listening and being a really good friend. God wants us to be great at things so we will thank Him and give Him the credit. Today in Large Group we're going to hear about some people who thought they were great but didn't want to give God the credit for it. Your mission is to look for clues to find out WHAT happened to those people and WHY."

© 2000 Willow Creek Community Church / Small Group Leader's Guidebook

SMALL GROUP (20 minutes)

REVIEW

ASK the kids, "Did you figure out WHAT happened to the Babylonians and WHY?" (*The Babylonians wanted to build a tower to their own greatness but they didn't want to give God the credit for their abilities. So, God mixed up their language so they couldn't understand each other and finish the tower and God scattered them across the earth.*)

TELL the kids, "We learned today that the Bible tells us the Lord God Almighty reigns (Revelation 19:6). That means we need to remember God is #1 and we need to give Him all the credit. Get it? (*Got it.*) Good!"

ACTIVITY: GET A CLUE! GAME.

The purpose of this game is to provide opportunities for children to practice giving God the credit. When playing the game, remember it can be easy to give God the credit when things are good, but it's much harder when things or circumstances are not so good. An example of this might be when they lose a game or don't make a good grade after they studied.

SUPPLIES PROVIDED BY YOUR ADMINISTRATOR

- One Get a Clue! Gameboard
- Who, What, Where/Character Cards — one per child
- Seven envelopes with a Solution Card or Try Again Card in each (Week 2)
- One Mystery Card (Week 2)
- Location Cards (Week 2)
- Pencils
- Playing pieces

SET UP

EXPLAIN to the children the goal of the game is to get a clue from different locations on the board in order to solve the mystery.

PASS to each player a pencil and a game piece.

HAVE each player choose a Who, What, Where/Character Card. This is who they will be for the game.

OPEN up the gameboard and place it in the center of the group.

PLACE the Secret Envelopes around the outside of the gameboard, then place the Location Cards face down on top of the corresponding Secret Envelope.

TELL the children, "Inside each envelope with either be a Solution Card to help solve the mystery or a Try Again Card."

HAVE the players place their game pieces at any location of their choice on the gameboard.

INSTRUCTIONS

READ the Mystery Card aloud to your group. "A week before Jenny's birthday she received a present in the mail. The card read, 'A special surprise for you!' In all the commotion of the week her present got misplaced and no one could seem to find it. Solve the mystery by finding out WHO sent the surprise, WHAT it is, and WHERE is it now."

PICK a player to start the game. Player starts by answering the question on the Location Card that corresponds to the location on the gameboard on which they placed their game piece.

AFTER answering the question, the child can be given the Secret Envelope

© 2000 Willow Creek Community Church / Small Group Leader's Guidebook

from that location. If they get an envelope with a Solution Card, they need to write it down on their Who What Where/Character Card and shouldn't let anyone see it. If they get a Try Again Card, they should not let anyone know what it says and then pretend to write something on their card.

PLAYERS can move from one location to any other when it is their turn.

FIRST one to correctly answer the Who, What, and Where mystery questions wins!

MYSTERY ANSWER: *Who:* Iffy Tiffy; *What:* Cookies; *Where:* Closet

WRAP UP

TELL the kids, "God gave us all special abilities and talents and He wants us to do our best at what we do! But we need to remember, just like the Babylonians needed to remember, that God reigns and is the one who deserves all the credit for the things we do, or say, or get. Even when we want to take all the credit for something, we can remember God is #1 and we need to give Him all the credit."

BIBLE VERSE

PASS out Bible Verse Cards and repeat together. "For our Lord God Almighty reigns." Revelation 19:6

PRAYER

Dear God,
We know that You are #1. You are Almighty. Help us to remember to give You the credit for all that we are able to do. Amen.

SHEPHERDING TIP: Incorporate some of what you learned about your kids in your prayer.

KID CONNECTION CONTINUES . . .

Small Group Leaders, this is a time for you and your group to: continue to build community, let your kids know you care about them and pray for them, hear their felt needs, and better equip you in knowing how to specifically reach out to each child.

Here are questions that might help you:
ASK the kids, "What is one of the best things that happened to you this week?"
ASK the kids, "What do you think will be one of your biggest challenges this week?"

© 2000 Willow Creek Community Church / Small Group Leader's Guidebook

Get a Clue!
God promises a Nation to Abram

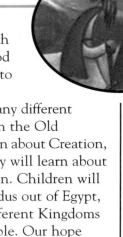

In the beginning when God made the whole earth and everything in it - God also created a beginning to His story. In these units children will learn the many different era's of God's story within the Old Testament. They will learn about Creation, the first families, and they will learn about God's promise of salvation. Children will then hear about the Exodus out of Egypt, the Conquests, God's different Kingdoms and the Exile of His people. Our hope within these lessons is to create a sequential view of the Old Testament to make a connection with how people and events fit together, as well as see how we can become part of God's story.

BIBLE STORY
Genesis 12:1-9
Our third "Get a Clue" lesson tells how God told Abram to leave the land of Haran. It probably didn't make sense to Abram to leave his home and friends, but Abram trusted and obeyed God. He set out for Canaan, taking his wife Sarai, his nephew Lot, and all their possessions. They stopped at the tree of Moreh at Shechem, and God promised to give the land to Abram's offspring. Abram built two altars along the journey to thank God.

KEY CONCEPT:
God is good so I can trust Him and obey even when I don't understand.

BIBLE VERSE
"He is good; His love endures forever." II Chronicles 5:13

OBJECTIVES
KNOW WHAT (LG): Children will hear the story of Abram and Sarai. They will learn how Abram followed God and how God promised to bless him and make a great nation from his family.
SO WHAT (LG): Children will learn that God is good and He wants to bless us.
NOW WHAT (SG): Children will be challenged to trust and obey God's commands even when they don't understand.

SPIRITUAL FORMATION
Trust/Obedience

IN ADVANCE DONE BY YOUR ADMINISTRATOR
• Photocopy the Situation Cards and Command Cards from the Get a Clue! Game Packet and cut out.
• Gather game pieces. Suggestions for game pieces: colored chips, colorful erasers, mini toy cars – one per child.
• Photocopy and cut apart Bible Verse Cards – one per child.
• Place the above-mentioned items along with the Get a Clue! Gameboard in a bin for each of the Small Group Leaders.

© 2000 Willow Creek Community Church / Small Group Leader's Guidebook

LEADER'S PREP

Sometimes God gives us commands that seem incomprehensible. Through His Word or the Holy Spirit, God asks us to do things we just don't understand. It's in the tension of that moment - between uncertainty and obedience - where our faith has the ability to either shine or fizzle out. Abram was a brilliant example of how to respond out of faith. He trusted God for what he could not see or understand. He knew that God was good. Because of that, Abram was able to trust God with all he had. As you read through Genesis 12:1-9 this week, ask God to show you how to trust Him even when you don't understand. Think about areas in your life where you need to say, "God is good so I can trust Him and obey."

KID CONNECTION (5 minutes)

WELCOME the children to Promiseland and tell them you are glad they are here. Introduce yourself again to your group and introduce any new kids.
ASK "What are some commands or rules you need to follow? Is it easy or difficult to follow them?"

TRANSITION
TELL the kids, "Today in Large Group we're going to hear about a man in the Bible who chose to follow God's commands even when it was really hard. See if you can discover who followed God and why it was so hard."

SMALL GROUP (20 minutes)

REVIEW
ASK the kids, "Who followed God?" (*Abram*) "Why was it hard?" (*He didn't know where he was going.*) "What did God promise him?" (*a large family, the land of Canaan, to make him a nation.*)
TELL the kids, "In the story we learned that Abram knew that God is good so he could trust Him and say 'yes' to His commands even when it was hard and he didn't understand. Today in Small Group we're going to play a game where we can practice saying 'yes' to God even when we don't understand."

ACTIVITY: GET A CLUE! GAME
The purpose of this game is for kids to practice obeying and recognizing God's commands in tough situations.

SUPPLIES PROVIDED BY YOUR ADMINISTRATOR
○ Get a Clue! Game (Week 3)

SET UP
EXPLAIN to the kids, "This game is a lot like the Get a Clue! Game we have been playing for the past two weeks. The goal of this game is to respond correctly to a given situation and move to the correct location. In this game, we will work

© 2000 Willow Creek Community Church / Small Group Leader's Guidebook

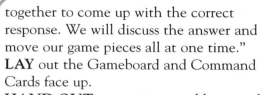

together to come up with the correct response. We will discuss the answer and move our game pieces all at one time."

LAY out the Gameboard and Command Cards face up.

HAND OUT game pieces and have each kid put his or her piece in the PARK.

INSTRUCTIONS

READ "Situation #1" card.

LOOK at the Command Cards to help you choose your answer. The Small Group Leader may have to explain what some of the Command Cards mean.

CHOOSE an answer to the question as a group, based on one of the Command Cards. The group may pick answer A, B, or C. All kids move their game pieces to the same place, according to the group answer. The Situation Card tells you where to move, based on your answer.

TELL the group members whether or not they landed in the correct location. If they did not, discuss the situation and talk about why their answer was incorrect. Encourage the kids to share what they would do if they would answer a situation differently than the options printed on the card.

READ "Situation #2" card and repeat instructions.

END the game when you have answered all the situation cards. The group wins if they landed in all the correct locations.

WRAP-UP

TELL the kids, "It's hard to do the right thing sometimes. Following God can be really hard when you don't understand His commands. But God loves you and knows what is best for you. He is good, so you can trust Him and obey His commands even when you don't understand, just like Abram."

BIBLE VERSE

PASS out the Bible Verse Card and repeat together: "He is good; His love endures forever." II Chronicles 5:13

SAY: "Get it?" (*Got it!*) "Good!"

PRAYER

Dear God,
Thank You for your love. Help us to trust and obey You even when it is hard or when we don't understand Your commands. Amen.

KID CONNECTION CONTINUES . . .

Small Group Leaders, this is a time for you and your group to: Continue to build community; let your kids know that you care and pray for them; and better equip

you with ways to reach out to each child and/or family.

ASK the kids, "What is one thing you wonder about God?"

© 2000 Willow Creek Community Church / Small Group Leader's Guidebook

Get a Clue!
God's Promise to Abraham and Sarah

In the beginning when God made the whole earth and everything in it, God also created a beginning to His story. In these upcoming lessons, children will learn the many different eras of God's story within the Old Testament. They will learn about Creation, the first families, and God's promise of salvation. Children will then hear about the Exodus out of Egypt, the Conquests, God's different Kingdoms and the exile of His people. Our hope within these lessons is to create a sequential view of the Old Testament to make a connection with how people and events fit together, as well as see how we can become part of God's story.

BIBLE STORY
Genesis 15:1-6; 17:1-8; 18:1-19; 21:1-6
This lesson continues the story of God's promise to Abram and Sarai. After spending their lives childless, they still trusted God to give them a son. God changed Abram's name to Abraham, meaning, "Father of many," and Sarai's name to Sarah, meaning "princess." Three visitors (angels, possibly God Himself) came to Abraham and confirmed that by the next year, Sarah would have a child. Sarah laughed, since she was past child-bearing age. The next year, when Abraham was one hundred years old, Sarah bore a child and named him Isaac, meaning, "he laughs."

BIBLE VERSE
"The Lord is faithful to all His promises."
Psalm 145:13

KEY CONCEPT:
God is a promise keeper so I can obey God and wait.

OBJECTIVES
KNOW WHAT (LG): Children will hear the story of Abraham and Sarah and how God promised them a son.
SO WHAT (LG): Children will learn that God is a Promise Keeper.
NOW WHAT (SG): Children will be challenged to trust and wait patiently for God to keep His promises to them.

SPIRITUAL FORMATION
Trust

IN ADVANCE DONE BY YOUR ADMINISTRATOR
- Acquire Get a Clue! Gameboard from the *Making It Connect* Curriculum Kit. (*One board per group.*)
- Photocopy the Character Cards/Who, What, Where Cards, Mystery Card, and Location Cards onto colored cardstock for Week 4 from the Get a Clue! Game Packet. Cut out each card. Each group needs only ONE Mystery Card.
- Make Secret Envelopes by gathering seven plain envelopes per group. Write one of the following locations on each of the envelopes: Home, School, Theater, Mall, Restaurant, Sports, Park. Photocopy and cut out the Solution

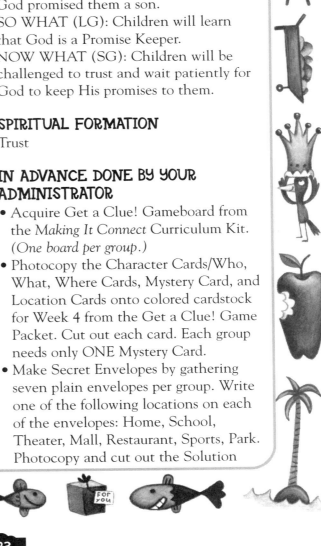

© 2000 Willow Creek Community Church / Small Group Leader's Guidebook

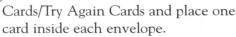

Cards/Try Again Cards and place one card inside each envelope.
- Gather game pieces. Suggestions: colored chips, erasers, candies, etc. (*one per child*)
- Photocopy Bible Verse Cards and cut apart – one per child. (*page 21 in Administrator's Guidebook.*)
- Place the above-mentioned items in a bin for each of the Small Group Leaders.

LEADER'S PREP

Read through Genesis 15-18; 21. Abraham and Sarah waited until they were one hundred years old for God to deliver on His promise to give them a child. No one likes to wait for anything, because waiting is hard! But, when we wait on God's promises, we can wait with the surety of fulfillment because God will keep His promises to us. It is in the "waiting" that God works on our character, our patience, and our ability to trust and believe Him. As you think through the things you are waiting for, ask yourself how you are doing in the "process" of waiting.

KID CONNECTION (5 minutes)

WELCOME the kids to Promiseland and share with them how glad you are that they are here.

TELL the kids about a time that someone made you a promise.

ASK the kids, "Has anyone ever promised you something? What was it? Did they keep that promise?"

TRANSITION

TELL the children, "Today, we're going to talk about promises. Sometimes people break promises, but God always keeps His promises. In Large Group we're going to be hearing about some people from the Bible who had to wait a long time for God to keep His promise. Your mission is to look for clues to find out WHO God made a promise to, WHAT promise was made, and HOW long they had to wait."

SMALL GROUP (20 minutes)

REVIEW

ASK the kids, "To whom did God make a promise?" (*Abraham & Sarah*) "What promise was made?" (*God promised them a son*) "Did God keep His promise?" (*Yes*)

TELL the kids, "It's really hard to wait for a promise to come true. And sometimes when we wait for so long, we begin to wonder if the promise is going to be kept! That's because people don't always keep their promises. But God is different. God is not like us. God will always keep His promises to us. Abraham had to wait a long time before he and Sarah had the son God promised them. Now, we are going to play a game. It teaches us that **GOD IS A PROMISE KEEPER SO WE CAN OBEY GOD AND WAIT.** Let's look at promises He has made to you and me."

ACTIVITY: GET A CLUE! GAME

The intention behind this game is for the kids to become aware of the many promises God makes to us.

© 2000 Willow Creek Community Church / Small Group Leader's Guidebook

SUPPLIES PROVIDED BY YOUR ADMINISTRATOR

- ○ Get a Clue! Gameboard
- ○ Character Cards/Who, What, Where Cards - one per child
- ○ Location Cards
- ○ Secret Envelopes with a Solution Card or Try Again Card in each *(Week 4)*
- ○ One Mystery Card *(Week 4)*
- ○ Game Pieces – one per child
- ○ Pencils
- ○ Bible Verse Cards

LEADER'S NOTES

1. *It will be very important for you to help the kids answer the promise questions.*
2. *Do not let anyone peek inside the Secret Envelopes ahead of time.*
3. *Location Card ANSWERS: If the promise is a people promise, there is no follow-up question. If the promise is a God promise, there is a follow-up question about God after the question.*
4. *You will know the right answer to the question by looking for a Scripture verse next to an answer. If there is a verse then it is God's promise.*
5. *Mystery ANSWER: Brains, 6:00 p.m., gym*

SET UP

EXPLAIN to the kids, "The goal of the game is for you to solve the mystery by correctly answering the promise questions on the Location Cards. A correct answer will earn you a clue from that location. The clues will help you solve the mystery."

LAY out the Gameboard.

PASS to each player a Character Card/Who, What, Where Card, a pencil, and a game piece.

READ the Mystery Card aloud.

PLACE the Location Cards face down by the game board.

PLACE the Secret Envelopes in front of the corresponding Location Cards.

TELL the kids, "In each envelope will either be clue to solve the mystery, or a Try Again. If there is a clue, write it on your Who, What, Where Card without anyone seeing. If there is no clue in the location, pretend like you're writing, or write down fake clues so no one else will know there's no clue in there. When you collect all three clues, you can solve the mystery. The first one to correctly solve the mystery wins!"

INSTRUCTIONS

HAVE each player start in any location.

PICK someone to start. That player chooses a location on the board and moves to that place. Leader picks a Location Card and reads it aloud. The player answers the question. If the player answers the question correctly, the leader hands the player the Secret Envelope. The player may look inside the envelope for clues to solve the mystery. If there is a clue to help solve the mystery, the player writes it on the Who, What, Where Card. If there is no clue, the player can pretend to write something so that the other players won't know if that Location has a clue to the solution. The leader then places the envelope back in front of them.

MOVE around the group giving each player an opportunity to move to a location and answer a question.

CONTINUE until the mystery is solved.

WRAP-UP

TELL the kids, "God makes so many wonderful promises to us! Today we've

© 2000 Willow Creek Community Church / Small Group Leader's Guidebook

only heard a few of them. One thing that is so wonderful about God is He will keep His promises to us no matter what! Even if we mess up and do the wrong thing, even if we forget about His promise to us, God will do what He says. Sometimes it takes a short time for God to keep His promises. Sometimes it might take a long time. Just like Abraham and Sarah, **WE CAN OBEY GOD AND WAIT BECAUSE HE IS A PROMISE KEEPER."**

BIBLE VERSE

PASS out verse card and repeat together. "The Lord is faithful to all His promises." Psalm 145:13

PRAYER

Dear God,
Thank You that You are a promise keeper. Thank You that we can always depend on You. Help us to obey You and trust that You will keep Your promises. Help us to be patient and wait for Your answers. Amen.

KID CONNECTION CONTINUES. . .

Small Group Leaders, this is a time for you and your group to: Continue to build community; let your kids know that you care and pray for them; and better equip you with ways to reach out to each child and/or family. Here are two questions that might help you:

ASK, "Did anything special happen to you this week?"
ASK, "Which one of God's promises is your favorite?"

© 2000 Willow Creek Community Church / Small Group Leader's Guidebook

Think Big
Unit 2 Overview

This is the second unit of the Promiseland year. In this unit, we are asking kids to "Think Big." We define this as thinking about things that are important to God. The first two weeks, Big Heart and Big Ten, will be spent studying the Ten Commandments. The next week's lesson, "Big Gift," is a presentation of the salvation message. The final week is called, "Big Thanks." In this lesson, we will study the story of Joshua and the people of Israel crossing the Jordan River, and learn about remembering to be thankful.

Lesson Overviews

Lesson 5

Big Heart for God: 10 Commandments (Exodus 19–20)

Key Concept: The Bible tells us how we can love God and live his way.

Bible Verse: "Love the Lord your God with all your heart and with all your soul and with all your mind." Matthew 22:37

Know What: Children will hear about the first four of the Ten Commandments that tell us how to love God.

So What: Children will learn that the Bible teaches us how God wants us to love Him and live His way.

Now What: Children will be challenged to remember the first four Commandments and think about ways they can apply them to their lives.

Lesson 6

The Big Ten: Ten Commandments (Exodus 19–20)

Key Concept: The Bible tells us how we can love God and love others.

Bible Verse: "Love your neighbor as yourself." Matthew 22:39

Know What: Children will hear how God gave the Ten Commandments to Moses and the people of Israel.

So What: Children will learn the Ten Commandments are God's way of telling us how to love Him and love others.

Now What: Children will play a game, helping them to learn the last six Commandments and apply them to their own lives.

Lesson 7

Big Gift (John 3:16)

Key Concept: God loves me and I can choose Him to be my forever friend.

Bible Verse: "For God so loved the world that He gave His one and only Son, that whoever believes in Him will not perish but have eternal life." John 3:16

Know What: Children will hear about God's love for them. They will learn they can choose to follow Him by Admitting their sin and asking for forgiveness, Believing in Jesus, and Choosing to follow God.

© 2000 Willow Creek Community Church / Small Group Leader's Guidebook

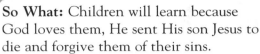

So What: Children will learn because God loves them, He sent His son Jesus to die and forgive them of their sins.

Now What: Children will hear their leader's testimony, and will have an opportunity to ask questions about what they learned in Large Group.

Lesson 8

Big Thanks: Joshua Crosses the Jordan River (Joshua 2–4)

Key Concept: God is good and I can remember to thank Him for what He has done.

Bible Verse: "Give thanks to the Lord, for He is good." Psalm 106:1

Objectives

Know What: Children will hear the story of how Joshua and the Israelites crossed the Jordan River, then built a monument to thank God for His goodness.

So What: Children will learn God is good.

Now What: Children will build their own monument of stones and be challenged to remember to thank God for the good things He has done.

Large Group Presentation Summary

These lessons are communicated using a storyboard, drama, and audience participation. Brightly-colored, fun props enhance the teaching area and make the lessons interesting and eye-catching. Like the first unit, repetition is used throughout the lessons to reinforce memory and comprehension.

Large Group Helpful Hints

1. You will need a storyboard for the first two weeks. To make a storyboard, cover a large bulletin board with black felt or black paper. The heart can be made of red posterboard or felt. Use pushpins to attach the heart to the storyboard.
2. Store the storyboard and heart carefully, as you will use them two weeks in a row.
3. Permission is granted to photocopy the optional drama in Lesson 5 and the drama in Lesson 6 for the actors in your program.
4. Lesson 5 asks for volunteers from the audience. Be sure to choose older kids who are comfortable reading aloud in front of a group.
5. Lesson 7 is a presentation of the Gospel message. This is a very special weekend, so create prayer teams and be sure everyone on your team is prepared.

Small Group Summary

In Small Group, children will think about the lessons they have learned and apply them to their lives. They will be thinking about real life situations. Weeks 5 and 6 use buckets and Ping-Pong balls to get kids thinking about the Ten Commandments. Week 7, salvation week, Small Group Leaders will share their own testimonies with their groups. Week 8, kids will create a "monument of thanks" to God.

© 2000 Willow Creek Community Church / Small Group Leader's Guidebook

Small Group Helpful Hints

1. Store Ping-Pong balls and buckets carefully, as you will use them more than once. Try to get colorful buckets. If budget or time is tight, you can use other small objects in place of the balls, such as erasers, rocks, toy people, or marbles.

2. Many places will donate the buckets. Try movie theaters and fast food restaurants.

3. Call the children in your group the week before lesson 7 to remind them to come. Or, think of fun ways to invite them, such as sending them a postcard in the mail or giving them a balloon with an invitation written on it.

4. During the Big Gift lesson, use God's Story cards only if kids need a prompt. If they are asking questions without the cards, you do not need to use them. Also, use the parent letter as a guide, then write your own on your own church's letterhead.

5. The "Leading Children to Christ" tape is in your *Making It Connect* curriculum kit. If you need additional tapes you can order them from the Willow Creek Association by calling 1-800-570-9812.

6. Don't forget to make use of the Shepherding Plan Guide to get to know the children in your Small Group. As time allows, pray specifically for prayer requests raised by children in your Small Group.

© 2000 Willow Creek Community Church / Small Group Leader's Guidebook

Think Big
Big Heart for God: The Ten Commandments

In the beginning when God made the whole earth and everything in it, God also created a beginning to His story. In these upcoming lessons, children will learn the many different eras of God's story within the Old Testament. They will learn about Creation, the first families, and God's promise of salvation. Children will then hear about the Exodus out of Egypt, the Conquests, God's different Kingdoms and the Exile of His people. Our hope within these lessons is to create a sequential view of the Old Testament to make a connection with how people and events fit together, as well as see how we can become part of God's story.

BIBLE STORY
Exodus 19–20
The people of Israel left Egypt, where they had been slaves for 40 years. They came out to the Desert of Sinai where they camped. Moses went up on Mount Sinai where God spoke to him. God said the people of Israel would be God's people set apart from the rest of the world. God gave Moses the Ten Commandments.

KEY CONCEPT: The Bible tells us how we can love God and live His way.

BIBLE VERSE
"Love the Lord your God with all your heart and with all your soul and with all your mind." Matthew 22:37

OBJECTIVES
KNOW WHAT (LG): Children will hear about the first four of the Ten Commandments that tell us how to love God.
SO WHAT (LG): Children will learn that the Bible teaches us how God wants us to love Him and live His way.
NOW WHAT (SG): Children will be challenged to remember the first four Commandments and think about ways that they can apply them to their lives.

SPIRITUAL FORMATION
Obedience

IN ADVANCE DONE BY YOUR ADMINISTRATOR
- Photocopy Commandment Cards and cut apart – one set per group (pages 23-24 in Administrator's Guidebook).
- Photocopy Situation Cards and cut apart – one set per group (page 25 in Administrator's Guidebook).
- Gather buckets – four per group. You can use plastic or metal buckets, fast food buckets, popcorn buckets, or something you already have on hand.
- Gather ping-pong balls – one per child.
- Photocopy Bible Verse Cards and cut apart – one per child (page 26 in Administrator's Guidebook).
- Place the items listed above into a bin for each Small Group Leader.

© 2000 Willow Creek Community Church / Small Group Leader's Guidebook

LEADER'S PREP

Read through Exodus 19–20. One of the most remarkable things about God is His steadfast nature. For example, God gave Moses and the Israelites the Ten Commandments for living life His way, and they still apply to us today. God's guidelines haven't changed for thousands of years! God wants us to love Him first, and then love people. The Ten Commandments show us how to do that. The first four Commandments show us how to love God and the last six Commandments show us how to love people. This week, you might take note of various ways you express your love to God by following His first four Commandments.

KID CONNECTION (5 minutes)

WELCOME kids to Promiseland and share with them how glad you are they are here.
SHARE with your group some things that are a big deal to you. (*friends, family, an activity*)
ASK the kids, "What are some things that are a big deal (*or important*) to you? Why are they a big deal?"

TRANSITION

TELL the kids, "Today in Large Group we are going to Think Big. That means that we are going to talk about things that are a big deal to God. We're going to learn about four things that are really important to Him. See if you can figure out and remember what those four things are."

SMALL GROUP (20 minutes)

REVIEW

TELL the kids, "In Large Group, we learned about things that are a big deal to God. We're going to do an activity and continue to 'Think Big' about how we can love God and live His way." (*Take out the Commandment Cards and place them in front of you with the Commandment number facing up.*)
ASK the kids, "What is the first Commandment?" (*Have no gods before me.*)
TURN over card #1 after their response.
REPEAT procedure with other three Commandment Cards.

ACTIVITY: The Top Four

The purpose of today's Small Group activity is for kids to learn and remember the first four of the Ten Commandments, and to think about how they can apply those Commandments to their lives.

SUPPLIES PROVIDED BY YOUR ADMINISTRATOR
- Commandment Cards
- Four Buckets
- Ping-Pong balls
- Situation Cards

© 2000 Willow Creek Community Church / Small Group Leader's Guidebook

SET-UP

PLACE the buckets in order one behind the other spacing them a foot apart. Put the correct Commandment Card, with number side up, next to each bucket. **HAVE** the kids stand in a single file line with the first person two feet away from the first bucket. **HAND** each player a ball just before they play.

INSTRUCTIONS: Part 1

EXPLAIN to the kids, "Each player must name the first Commandment and then throw the ball into bucket #1. If you name the Commandment and make the bucket, you move on to naming the second Commandment and throwing the ball into the second bucket. You have two tries to make the bucket. Your turn ends when you do not make the bucket or when you cannot name the Commandment." **ROTATE** kids through the game until everyone gets a turn.

INSTRUCTIONS: Part 2

MOVE the buckets so they are two inches apart and have your group sit in a circle around them. **TELL** your group, "I'm going to read a situation that describes how you can

follow the Commandments we learned about today. You need to figure out which one of the first four Commandments I'm describing. When you decide on a Commandment, throw your ball into the correct bucket (1, 2, 3, or 4)." **GIVE** each kid one ping-pong ball. **READ** the Situation Cards one at a time. When you have read all the Situation Cards, you are done with the game.

WRAP-UP

TELL the kids, "God made you and He loves you! He knows that life is at its best when we follow Him and His commands. That's why He gave us the first four Commandments, so we could know how to love Him and live His way."

BIBLE VERSE

PASS OUT Bible Verse Cards and repeat the verse together. "Love the Lord your God with all your heart, and with all your soul and with all your mind." Matthew 22:37

PRAYER

Dear God,
Thank You that You care about us so much that You have told us the best way to live. Please help us to love You by following these Commandments. Amen.

KID CONNECTION CONTINUES . . .

Small Group leaders, this is a time for you and your group to: continue to build community, let your kids know that you care and pray for them, and better equip you with ways to reach out to each child and/or family.

ASK, "What was the biggest, most important thing that happened in your life this past week?"

© 2000 Willow Creek Community Church / Small Group Leader's Guidebook

Think Big
The Big Ten: Commandments 5-10

In the beginning when God made the whole earth and everything in it, God also created a beginning to His story. In these upcoming lessons, children will learn the many different eras of God's story within the Old Testament. They will learn about Creation, the first families, and God's promise of salvation. Children will then hear about the Exodus out of Egypt, the Conquests, God's different Kingdoms and the Exile of His people. Our hope within these lessons is to create a sequential view of the Old Testament, to make a connection with how people and events fit together, as well as see how we can become part of God's story.

BIBLE STORY

Exodus 19-20
The third month after the people of Israel left Egypt, they came to the Desert of Sinai. The people of Israel camped there at the base of Mount Sinai. God told Moses, their leader, that they were to be His treasured nation. God came to Mount Sinai in a cloud of thunder, lightning, and fire. He called Moses to meet Him at the top of Mount Sinai. There, He gave Moses the Ten Commandments.

KEY CONCEPT: The Bible tells us how we can love God and love others.

BIBLE VERSE

"Love your neighbor as yourself." Matthew 22:39

OBJECTIVES

KNOW WHAT (LG): Children will hear how God gave the Ten Commandments to Moses and the people of Israel.
SO WHAT (LG): Children will learn that the Bible tells us how to love others and live His way.
NOW WHAT (SG): Children will play a game that will help them learn the ten Commandments, identify ways they can follow them, and learn how each command helps us to love others.

SPIRITUAL FORMATION

Obedience

IN ADVANCE DONE BY YOUR ADMINISTRATOR

• Gather buckets – six per group
• Gather Ping-Pong balls – one per child
• Photocopy Commandment Cards and cut apart – one set per group (*page 27 in Administrator's Guidebook*).
• Photocopy Bible Verse Cards and cut apart – one per child (*page 28 in Administrator's Guidebook*).
• Place the above-mentioned items into a bin for each Small Group Leader.

LEADER'S PREP

Read Matthew 22:34-40. Jesus said we are to love God with our heart, soul and mind. The first four of the Ten Commandments show us how to do that.

© 2000 Willow Creek Community Church / Small Group Leader's Guidebook

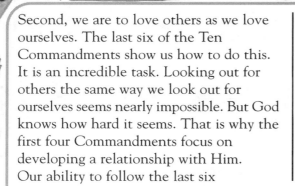

Second, we are to love others as we love ourselves. The last six of the Ten Commandments show us how to do this. It is an incredible task. Looking out for others the same way we look out for ourselves seems nearly impossible. But God knows how hard it seems. That is why the first four Commandments focus on developing a relationship with Him. Our ability to follow the last six commandments are determined by our willingness to follow the first four. If we don't love God first, we will fail at loving others. If we love God first, we are able to do as He asks. Which of the last six Commandments are most difficult for you to follow? Pray for God to strengthen you. Then, pick one day this week to focus on actively loving others, putting their needs before your own.

KID CONNECTION (5 minutes)

WELCOME the kids to Promiseland and tell them you are glad they are here.
ASK your group, "What are some rules you have to follow at home, at school, or with your family? Why do you think we have rules?"

TRANSITION
TELL your group, "Rules are meant to help us. Some keep us from getting hurt, some keep order, and some help us show kindness to others. Today in Large Group, we're going to continue learning about God's 'Big Ten' – the Ten Commandments. Today we will be learning about the last six Commandments – which are all about how to love other people."

SMALL GROUP (20 minutes)

REVIEW
TELL the kids, "In Large Group, we learned that the Bible tells us how to love others and live His way. Now, we are going to play a game that will take what we've learned and put it into practice in our everyday lives. This game is similar to the one we played last week."

ACTIVITY: The Big Ten Game
The purpose of this lesson is to have kids learn, apply, and understand how they can love others.

SUPPLIES PROVIDED BY YOUR ADMINISTRATOR
○ Six Buckets
○ Ping-Pong balls
○ Commandment Cards

SET-UP
HAVE your group sit in two lines facing each other.
SET the buckets in a row between the two lines of kids.
LAY one Commandment Card in front of each bucket.
GIVE one Ping-Pong ball to each group member.

© 2000 Willow Creek Community Church / Small Group Leader's Guidebook

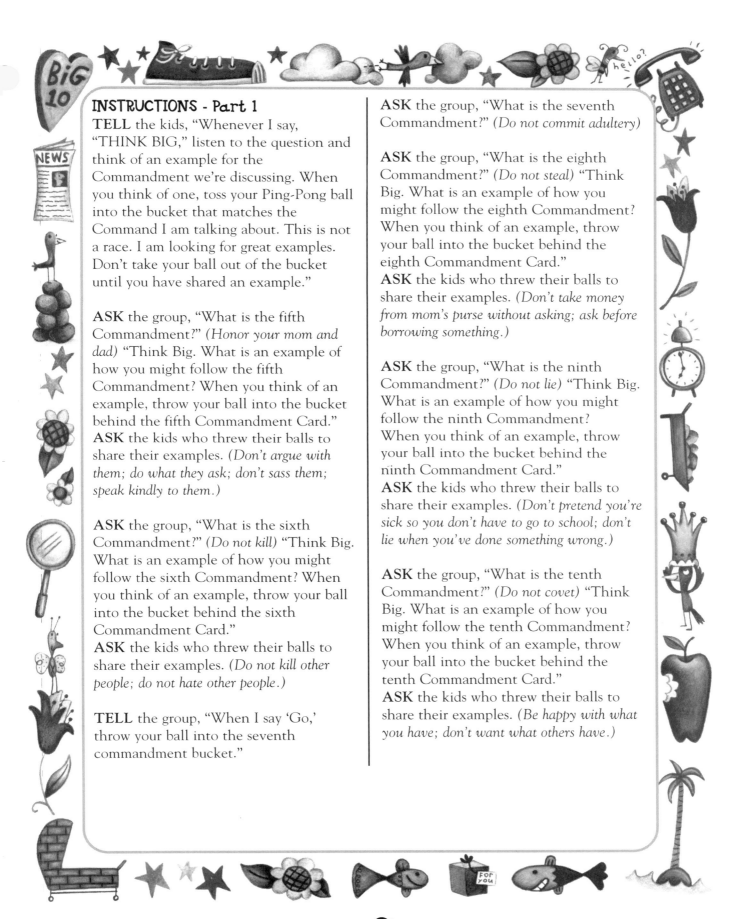

INSTRUCTIONS - Part 1

TELL the kids, "Whenever I say, "THINK BIG," listen to the question and think of an example for the Commandment we're discussing. When you think of one, toss your Ping-Pong ball into the bucket that matches the Command I am talking about. This is not a race. I am looking for great examples. Don't take your ball out of the bucket until you have shared an example."

ASK the group, "What is the fifth Commandment?" (*Honor your mom and dad*) "Think Big. What is an example of how you might follow the fifth Commandment? When you think of an example, throw your ball into the bucket behind the fifth Commandment Card."
ASK the kids who threw their balls to share their examples. (*Don't argue with them; do what they ask; don't sass them; speak kindly to them.*)

ASK the group, "What is the sixth Commandment?" (*Do not kill*) "Think Big. What is an example of how you might follow the sixth Commandment? When you think of an example, throw your ball into the bucket behind the sixth Commandment Card."
ASK the kids who threw their balls to share their examples. (*Do not kill other people; do not hate other people.*)

TELL the group, "When I say 'Go,' throw your ball into the seventh commandment bucket."

ASK the group, "What is the seventh Commandment?" (*Do not commit adultery*)

ASK the group, "What is the eighth Commandment?" (*Do not steal*) "Think Big. What is an example of how you might follow the eighth Commandment? When you think of an example, throw your ball into the bucket behind the eighth Commandment Card."
ASK the kids who threw their balls to share their examples. (*Don't take money from mom's purse without asking; ask before borrowing something.*)

ASK the group, "What is the ninth Commandment?" (*Do not lie*) "Think Big. What is an example of how you might follow the ninth Commandment? When you think of an example, throw your ball into the bucket behind the ninth Commandment Card."
ASK the kids who threw their balls to share their examples. (*Don't pretend you're sick so you don't have to go to school; don't lie when you've done something wrong.*)

ASK the group, "What is the tenth Commandment?" (*Do not covet*) "Think Big. What is an example of how you might follow the tenth Commandment? When you think of an example, throw your ball into the bucket behind the tenth Commandment Card."
ASK the kids who threw their balls to share their examples. (*Be happy with what you have; don't want what others have.*)

© 2000 Willow Creek Community Church / Small Group Leader's Guidebook

INSTRUCTIONS - Part 2

TELL the kids, "The Big Ten show us how to love God and love others. Why does God want us to follow the last six Commandments? *(He wants us to love others.)* Let's talk about all the good things that happen when we love others His way. Again, when I say, "Think Big," think of an example. When you have one, throw your ball into the bucket. Ready?"

ASK the group, "Think Big. What good things happen when we follow the eighth Commandment?" *(people are not angry with each other, build trust)*

ASK the group, "Think Big. What good things happen when we follow the fifth Commandment?" *(do not hurt our parents' feelings, parents give us privileges)*

ASK the group, "Think Big. What good things happen when we follow the ninth Commandment?" *(build trust, clear conscience)*

WRAP-UP

TELL the kids, "God knows you and He loves you. God also created you and that's why He knows what's best for you. God gave us the Ten Commandments to help us have the BEST life. That's why He wants us to always 'Think Big' about how we love other people. Next week we're going to learn about the biggest and best gift God ever gave us. Be here next week when we find out what the Big Gift was! You won't want to miss it!"

BIBLE VERSE

PASS OUT Bible Verse Cards and repeat the verse together. "Love your neighbor as yourself." Matthew 22:39

REMIND the kids, "This verse means we are to love other people with as much care and concern as we love ourselves."

PRAYER

Dear God, You are so wonderful. Thank You for giving us the Ten Commandments, so we can learn to love others and live Your way. Thank You that You know the best way for us to live. Please help us to love You and love others more each day. Amen.

KID CONNECTION CONTINUES . . .

Small Group Leaders, this is a time for you and your group to: continue to build community, let your kids know that you care and pray for them, and better equip you with ways to know how to reach out to each child and/or family.

Here are two questions that might help you: What is the best gift you have ever given to someone?
What is the best gift you have ever received?

© 2000 Willow Creek Community Church / Small Group Leader's Guidebook

Think Big
Big Gift: Salvation

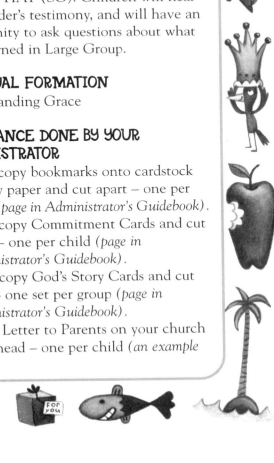

In the beginning when God made the whole earth and everything in it, God also created a beginning to His story. In these upcoming lessons, children will learn the many different eras of God's story within the Old Testament. They will learn about Creation, the first families, and God's promise of salvation. Children will then hear about the Exodus out of Egypt, the Conquests, God's different Kingdoms and the Exile of His people. Our hope within these lessons is to create a sequential view of the Old Testament to make a connection with how people and events fit together, as well as see how we can become part of God's story.

BIBLE STORY

John 3:16
In today's lesson children will be asked to "Think Big" about God and what God thinks is important. Children will hear how God loves them, and wants us to choose Him to be our Forever Friend. They will hear the following points: God is perfect, He loves them, sin is the problem, and Jesus paid for their sins. Then, they will be asked if they would like to make God their forever friend.

**KEY CONCEPT:
God loves me and I can choose Him to be my forever friend.**

BIBLE VERSE

"For God so loved the world that He gave His one and only Son, that whoever

believes in Him will not perish but have eternal life."
John 3:16

OBJECTIVES

KNOW WHAT (LG): Children will hear about God's love for them. They will learn they can choose to follow Him by Admitting their sin and asking for forgiveness, Believing in Jesus, and Choosing to follow God.
SO WHAT (LG): Children will learn that because God loves them, He sent His son Jesus to die and forgive them of their sins.
NOW WHAT (SG): Children will hear their leader's testimony, and will have an opportunity to ask questions about what they learned in Large Group.

SPIRITUAL FORMATION

Understanding Grace

IN ADVANCE DONE BY YOUR ADMINISTRATOR

- Photocopy bookmarks onto cardstock quality paper and cut apart – one per child (*page in Administrator's Guidebook*).
- Photocopy Commitment Cards and cut apart – one per child (*page in Administrator's Guidebook*).
- Photocopy God's Story Cards and cut apart– one set per group (*page in Administrator's Guidebook*).
- Write Letter to Parents on your church letterhead – one per child (*an example*

© 2000 Willow Creek Community Church / Small Group Leader's Guidebook

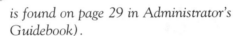

is found on page 29 in *Administrator's Guidebook*).

• Put supplies in a bin for each Small Group Leader.

LEADER'S PREP

Salvation weekend is one of the most important weekends of the year. You get a chance to see God actively move in the lives of children. Better yet, you get to play a part in helping them become part of God's family. This week as you prepare, spend some time praying for the message to be communicated, for each child's attentiveness, and responsiveness, and for the teacher and Small Group Leaders to communicate clearly so kids will make the choice to ask God to be their forever friend. Also, pray and prepare for how you will share your own testimony. Listen to the cassette tape, "How To Lead a Child to Christ," included in the *Making It Connect* Curriculum Kit.

KID CONNECTION (5 minutes)

WELCOME the kids and tell them you are glad they are here.
ASK the kids, "Do you remember the Ten Commandments? List them for me." (*Have no gods before Me, Have no idols, Don't misuse god's name, Keep the Sabbath holy, Honor your mom and dad, Do not murder, Do not commit adultery, Do not steal, Do not lie, Do not covet*) "Has it been hard to follow the Ten Commandments?" (*yes*) "Why do you suppose it is hard?"

(*I like doing wrong things; sometimes it is easier to do the wrong thing.*)

TRANSITION
TELL the kids, "When we break God's Commandments, it is called sin. The Bible tells us that everyone has sinned. Sin is a big deal to God, so He gave us a Big Gift to take care of sin. Listen in Large Group to see what Big Gift God gave us."

SMALL GROUP (20 minutes)

REVIEW
ASK the kids, "So, what was the Big Gift? (*Jesus*) God cares about us so much that He sent His son Jesus to take our punishment for us. That's awesome and amazing! **GOD LOVES YOU, SO YOU CAN CHOOSE HIM TO BE YOUR FOREVER FRIEND.**"

SUPPLIES PROVIDED BY YOUR ADMINISTRATOR
○ Bookmarks – one per child
○ Commitment Cards – one per child
○ God's Story Cards – one set per group
○ Letter to Parents – one per child

© 2000 Willow Creek Community Church / Small Group Leader's Guidebook

NOTES TO LEADER

The intention of this time is to review and ask questions about what the kids learned today in Large Group. Whether a child is already a Christian or not, this will be an important time for each child to either learn for the first time, or to re-affirm what they already know about God's forgiveness.

Because the kids look to you as their leader, it is important for you to authentically share your testimony in a manner they will understand.

TESTIMONY GUIDE: Review your story using these three guidelines:

1. (BC) Where were you spiritually before receiving Christ? What were you like? What caused you to consider God/Jesus?
2. (t) What realization did you come to that finally motivated you to make Jesus your forever friend? Specifically, remind the kids how you Admitted, Believed, and Chose to become a Christian.
3. (AD) How did your life begin to change after becoming a Christian?

ACTIVITY 1: LEADER'S STORY

GATHER your group and sit in a circle.
SHARE how you came to ask Jesus to be your Forever Friend by using the guide above.

ACTIVITY 2: GOD'S STORY

TAKE out the God's Story Cards. Put the "God's Story" Card in the center of your group. Keep the rest of the cards face down in your lap.
TELL the kids, "For some of you, this is the first time you are hearing about how to become a Christian. Some of you are already Christians, so this is a review. Either way, take this time to learn God's story so you can remember it and share it with friends and family. Let's review the story, and if you have any questions about the cards, feel free to ask as we go."

TURN over GOD card.
ASK, "What does it mean?" (*God is perfect*)
"What is God like?" (*God is loving, kind, fair, holy, and perfect*)
"Do you have any questions about what you heard today about God?"
TURN over HEART card.
ASK, "What did you learn today about God's love?" (*He loves me.*)
"Were you wondering anything about God's love?"
TURN over WORLD card.
ASK, "What did you learn today about sin?" (*Sin is the problem.*)
"What did you learn about how we are different from God?" (*God is perfect and we sin.*)
"What does sin do?" (*Sin separates us from God.*)
"What happens when you sin after you become a Christian?" (*No matter how much you sin, you will always be a part of God's family.*)
"Do you have any questions about sin?"
TURN over CROSS card.
ASK, "What did you learn today about Jesus?" (*Jesus paid for my sin.*)
"Why did Jesus die on the cross?" (*To take the punishment for my sins, so God wouldn't see our sins any more*)
"Do you ever wonder anything about Jesus?"
TURN over A.B.C. card.
ASK, "What does A.B.C. stand for?" (*A-Admit your sins, B-Believe in Jesus, and C-Choose to follow Him forever.*)

© 2000 Willow Creek Community Church / Small Group Leader's Guidebook

WRAP-UP

TELL the kids, "If you asked God to be your forever friend, tell your parents about that decision. If you have more questions, you can ask your parents, me, or anyone from here in Promiseland."

PASS OUT the Commitment Cards and ask the kids to listen carefully as you read three statements.

- Today for the first time I prayed to ask for God's forgiveness and for Him to be my Forever Friend.
- I already prayed to ask God for His forgiveness and for Him to be my Forever Friend.
- I want to think more about it.

HAVE the kids mark one box and fill out their information on the other side of the card.

EXPLAIN to the kids, "If you asked God to be your forever friend today, or if you have done that in the past, you are now in God's family forever. If you did not pray today, God still loves you and wants to be your forever friend. You can take this step whenever you are ready."

PASS out the bookmarks.

TELL the kids, "**GOD LOVES YOU AND YOU CAN CHOOSE HIM TO BE YOUR FOREVER FRIEND.** If you prayed for the first time today, or if you already prayed, write your name and date on the bookmark."

BIBLE VERSE

PASS OUT Bible Verse Cards. "For God so loved the world that He gave His one and only Son, that whoever believes in Him will not perish but have eternal life." John 3:16

REMIND the kids, "This verse tells us that God has done His part; now, you can ask Him to be your forever friend."

PRAYER

Dear God, Thank You for sending Jesus to die on the cross. Thank You for Your Big Gift. Help us to love You more each day. Amen.

LARGE GROUP CELEBRATION (10 minutes)

RETURN to Large Group for a music celebration!

TALLY the responses from the Commitment Cards on to one blank Commitment Card. Give that Commitment Card to your Administrator. Save your kids' Commitment Cards for yourself.

© 2000 Willow Creek Community Church / Small Group Leader's Guidebook

Think Big
Big Thanks: Crossing the Jordan

In the beginning when God made the whole earth and everything in it, God also created a beginning to His story. In these upcoming lessons, children will learn the many different eras of God's story within the Old Testament. They will learn about Creation, the first families, and God's promise of salvation. Children will then hear about the Exodus out of Egypt, the Conquests, God's different Kingdoms and the Exile of His people. Our hope within these lessons is to create a sequential view of the Old Testament to make a connection with how people and events fit together, as well as see how we can become part of God's story.

BIBLE STORY

Joshua 3–4

When Moses died, God chose Joshua to lead the people of Israel. God promised to give the city of Jericho to the Israelites, so Joshua sent spies into the city. When they returned, they told Joshua that the people of Jericho were fearful. Joshua and the people of Israel needed to cross the Jordan River to get there. God stopped the flow of the Jordan and piled up water on each side of a dry walkway through the river. The Israelites were able to cross. Then, after they crossed the Jordan, Joshua and the Israelites built an monument out of stones in order to thank God, and remember how good He had been to them.

BIBLE VERSE

"Give thanks to the Lord, for He is good."
Psalm 106:1

KEY CONCEPT:
God is good and I can remember to thank Him for what He has done.

OBJECTIVES

KNOW WHAT (LG): Children will hear the story of how Joshua and the Israelites crossed the Jordan River, then built a monument to thank Him for His goodness.
SO WHAT (LG): Children will learn that God is good.
NOW WHAT (SG): Children will build their own monument of stones and be challenged to remember to thank God for the good things He has done.

SPIRITUAL FORMATION

Thankfulness

IN ADVANCE DONE BY YOUR ADMINISTRATOR

• Photocopy Bible Verse Cards and cut apart – one per child (*page 35 in Administrator's Guidebook*).
• Gather stones - one per child. Stones should be about four inches wide, and smooth enough for kids to write on. You will find them at landscaping and garden centers.
• Gather pens and markers – several per group. Ballpoint gel pens work best on the stones. You will find them at craft and hobby stores.
• Place the above-mentioned items into a

© 2000 Willow Creek Community Church / Small Group Leader's Guidebook

bin for each Small Group Leader.

LEADER'S PREP
Read Joshua 2–4. God is good. He is faithful to us all the time. When trouble comes, it is easy for us to forget God's track record of thousands of years of faithfulness. Throughout the Exodus, the Israelites forgot God's faithfulness many times. However, when they crossed the Jordan River, they built a monument to thank God. This would help them remember to be thankful in the future, even during the hard times. This week, think about things for which you are thankful. You might make a list and keep it handy as a reminder to thank God. Think of a story of God's goodness in your life that would be appropriate to share with the kids in your Small Group.

KID CONNECTION (5 minutes)

WELCOME the kids to Promiseland and tell them you are glad they came.
ASK the kids, "What are you thankful for?"

TRANSITION
TELL your group, "Today in Large Group, we will hear a story about remembering to be thankful. When you come back to Small Group, tell me what the people did so they would remember to thank God."

SMALL GROUP (20 minutes)

REVIEW
ASK the kids, "What did the people of Israel do so they would remember to thank God?" (*They built a monument out of stones from the Jordan River.*)

ACTIVITY: Monument of Thanks
The purpose of today's Small Group activity is for kids to remember the things God has given them or done for them, and identify ways that they can remember to thank God in the future.

SUPPLIES PROVIDED BY YOUR ADMINISTRATOR
○ Stones – one per child
○ Pens and markers

PART ONE
TELL your group, "We are going to build a monument of thanks, just like the Israelites did in the story we heard today."
PASS each kid one stone.
BEGIN by sharing a story about something for which you are thankful to God. After you share your story, put your stone in the middle of the circle.
SAY, "Now, think about your own life. What are you thankful for? If you'd like, you can share a story about something for which you are thankful. When you do, you can put your stone in the middle of the circle with mine. When we're finished, we will have a monument of thanks to God."

© 2000 Willow Creek Community Church / Small Group Leader's Guidebook

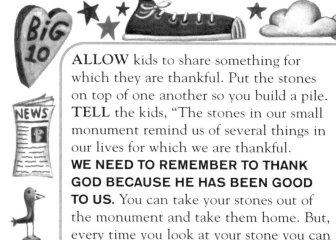

ALLOW kids to share something for which they are thankful. Put the stones on top of one another so you build a pile. TELL the kids, "The stones in our small monument remind us of several things in our lives for which we are thankful. **WE NEED TO REMEMBER TO THANK GOD BECAUSE HE HAS BEEN GOOD TO US.** You can take your stones out of the monument and take them home. But, every time you look at your stone you can remember what God has done for you, and what He did for the people of Israel."

PART TWO

EXPLAIN to the kids, "We're going to make these stones into 'thankful reminders' for you to take home."
PUT the pens or markers in the middle of the circle.

TELL the kids, "Remember that thing you said you are thankful for? Write something on your stone that will help you remember to be thankful. You can write a name, draw a picture, or write a sentence on your stone that will remind you of God's goodness."

WRAP-UP

TELL the kids: "It is easy to forget that **GOD IS GOOD, AND WE SHOULD THANK HIM FOR WHAT HE HAS DONE IN OUR LIVES.** We need help to remember! That's why God wanted Joshua and the Israelites to pick up stones from the sea. God knew that they needed help to remember what He did for them. God also wants us to remember that He has been good to us. This week, I challenge you to come up with your own 'thankful reminder' so you remember to thank God."

BIBLE VERSE

PASS OUT verse card and repeat verse together. "Give thanks to the Lord for He is good." Psalm 106:1
REMIND the kids, "This verse is exactly what we have talked about today. We must thank God, because He is good."

PRAYER

Dear God,
Thank You for loving us. Thank You for giving us memories, so we can remember all the wonderful things in our lives. Help us to remember that no matter what we are going though, You are good and You deserve our thanks. Amen.

KID CONNECTION CONTINUES . . .

Small Group Leaders, this is a time for you and your group to: continue to build community, let your kids know that you care and pray for them, and better equip you with ways to know how to reach out to each child and/or family.

ASK, "If you could be great at any one thing, what would it be?"

© 2000 Willow Creek Community Church / Small Group Leader's Guidebook

Unit 3 Overview
Tell Me A Story

Unit Summary

This third and final unit of this quarter completes a sequential journey through the Old Testament. The stories included are exciting, action-filled accounts about important people of the Old Testament. The lessons focus on deepening kids' relationships with God. Kids will learn about prayer and Bible reading, confession of sin, making God first priority, loving God wholeheartedly, and standing up for God.

Lesson Overviews

Lesson 9
Samuel and Eli (I Samuel 3)
Key Concept: God communicates to us so I can listen and talk to Him.
Bible Verse: "The Lord will hear when I call to Him." Psalm 4:3
Know What: Children will hear the story of God calling out to Samuel.
So What: Children will learn God communicates with us.
Now What: Children will consider ways they can spend time reading God's word, listening and praying to God.

Lesson 10
David's Heart (I Samuel 16; I Kings 2:1-4)
Key Concept: God wants us to love Him with all our hearts.
Bible Verse: "Man looks at the outward appearance, but the Lord looks at the heart." I Samuel 16:7
Know What: Children will hear how David was a man who loved, trusted, and followed God.
So What: Children will learn God wants us to love Him with all our hearts.
NOW WHAT: Children will be challenged to love God with their whole hearts.

Lesson 11
Elijah and Baal (I Kings 18:16-39)
Key Concept: – God is the One True God and I can choose to follow only Him.
Bible Verse: "You shall have no other Gods before me." Exodus 20:3
Know What: Children will hear the story of how God showed Himself as the One True God when Elijah and the prophets of Baal had a contest on Mount Carmel.
So What: Children will learn God is the only true God.
Now What: Children will identify ways they can choose to follow God.

© 2000 Willow Creek Community Church / Small Group Leader's Guidebook

Lesson 12

Jonah (Jonah 1–3)

Key Concept: God is forgiving and I can go to Him every time I sin and ask for forgiveness.

Bible Verse: "If we confess our sins He is faithful and just and will forgive us our sins." I John 1:9

Know What: Children will hear the story of Jonah running from God. After turning back to God, God forgave him and gave him another chance to go to Nineveh and deliver God's message.

So What: Children will learn that God is forgiving and wants us to go to Him every time we sin.

Now What: Children will identify times that they can go to God and ask for forgiveness.

Lesson 13

Shadrach, Meshach, and Abednego (Daniel 3:1-30)

Key Concept: Believing in the One True God means standing up for Him.

Bible Verse: "Be strong in the Lord and in His mighty power." Ephesians 6:10

Know What: Children will hear the story of Shadrach, Meshach, and Abednego and how they stood up for God by not worshipping idols even if it meant they might die in a furnace.

So What: Children will learn believing in the One True God means standing up for Him.

Now What: Children will be challenged to think of ways they can stand up for God in their lives.

Large Group Presentation Summary

This unit uses a traditional storytelling format with a twist – drama! These dramas are casual and fun. The first two lessons will be presented by your team. The last three lessons in this unit are on video.

Large Group Helpful Hints

1. The first two lessons in this unit require more preparation than usual, so you will want to plan ahead. View the video to get ideas on how to present the first two dramas.

2. Plan to use a TV/VCR for the last three lessons.

3. Actors come on stage in normal clothes and put on costumes while they talk to the audience. Actors should wear all black, or decide on appropriate colors to wear under costumes. Costumes should be simple robes or smocks, quick and easy to put on in front of the audience.

4. Arrange rehearsals, and be sure actors have memorized their lines.

5. If you are normally in a classroom-type space, reserve a larger space if possible with a stage or large teaching area for the first two lessons in this Unit.

6. Because of the storytelling nature of these dramas, anyone can play any part. A teenaged girl can play Eli with the right costuming. Use Junior High students through adults.

7. In order to save time and resources, use the same library props, costumes, and large storybook for Lessons 9 and 10.

© 2000 Willow Creek Community Church / Small Group Leader's Guidebook

Small Group Summary

In Small Group, kids will start to apply the truths they have learned in Large Group. In Lesson 9, they will write out a prayer to God. In lesson 10, they will play a game called Heart Skip and Jump, where they will think about loving God. In Lesson 11, they will write a story about themselves in comic strip form, depicting a time they followed God. In Lesson 12 they will examine sin in their lives, and in Lesson 13 they will play a memory game about standing up for God.

Small Group Helpful Hints

1. Lesson 9 requires looking up Bible verses. Instructions are given on how to look up a verse. Don't race through this section. If you need to, take a few extra minutes to be sure each child understands the instructions. Have Bibles in the same version available for children to use.

2. This unit requires a lot of drawing or writing. If your group sits on the floor, cut pieces of cardboard or gather backs of writing paper tablets, so children have a smooth, solid surface to write on.

3. These Lessons focus on a relationship with God. If a new child is hesitant to participate, don't force them. Let them observe the group.

4. Don't forget to make use of the Shepherding Plan Guide to get to know the children in your Small Group. As time allows, pray specifically for prayer requests raised by children in your Small Group.

© 2000 Willow Creek Community Church / Small Group Leader's Guidebook

Tell Me a Story
Samuel and Eli

In the beginning when God made the whole earth and everything in it, God also created a beginning to His story. In these upcoming lessons, children will learn the many different eras of God's story within the Old Testament. They will learn about Creation, the first families, and God's promise of salvation. Children will then hear about the Exodus out of Egypt, the Conquests, God's different Kingdoms and the Exile of His people. Our hope within these lessons is to create a sequential view of the Old Testament to make a connection with how people and events fit together, as well as see how we can become part of God's story.

BIBLE STORY

I Samuel 3

Samuel was a boy who lived with a priest named Eli. Late one night, God called out to Samuel. Samuel thought it was Eli calling him, and went down to Eli's room. This happened twice more. After the third time, Eli realized God was calling to Samuel. He told Samuel that when God spoke again, he was to say, "Speak, Lord, for your servant is listening." So Samuel did as Eli said, and God spoke to him that night.

KEY CONCEPT
God communicates to us so I can listen and talk to Him.

BIBLE VERSE

"The Lord will hear when I call to Him." Psalm 4:3

OBJECTIVES

KNOW WHAT (LG): Children will hear the story of God calling out to Samuel.
SO WHAT (LG): Children will learn God communicates with us.
NOW WHAT (SG): Children will consider ways they can spend time reading God's word, listening and praying to God.

SPIRITUAL FORMATION

Reading God's Word/Praying

IN ADVANCE DONE BY YOUR ADMINISTRATOR

- Photocopy DATA Letters – one per child (*page 37 in Administrator's Guidebook*).
- Photocopy Bible Verse Cards and cut apart – one per child (*page 36 in Administrator's Guidebook*).
- Gather Bibles – one for every two children.
- Gather markers – each Small Group should have a variety.
- Place the above-mentioned items into a bin for each Small Group Leader.

© 2000 Willow Creek Community Church / Small Group Leader's Guidebook

LEADER'S PREP

The story of Samuel and Eli is intriguing. God called out not just once or twice, but three times to Samuel by name. Each time Samuel woke up, he thought Eli the Priest was calling for him. He had no idea the God of the universe was calling his name until being prompted by Eli. It took Samuel a long time to realize God was calling, but when he did, he was ready to listen. How many times does God call us by name and we don't recognize His voice? This week as you read I Samuel 3, listen for God to call your name. In the grocery store, at work, at church, or in your home, listen to God. Don't miss what He wants to say to you.

KID CONNECTION (5 minutes)

WELCOME the kids and tell them you are glad they are here.
TELL the kids, "Pretend like you have a really important message to tell your very best friend. What are ten different ways that you could give your friend the message?" (*Talk, write a letter, e-mail, sing, draw, act it out, hand gestures*)

TRANSITION

TELL your group, "There are many different ways we can communicate with people other than talking. We can write things down, draw pictures, or use our hands and voices to tell them what we are trying to say. Today in Large Group, we're going to learn about some of the ways God communicates with us. Listen for one way you can communicate with God."

SMALL GROUP (20 minutes)

REVIEW

ASK the kids, "Did you figure out how God communicated to Samuel? (*He spoke to Samuel out loud.*) "What is one way God communicates with us today?" (*Through the Bible*)
SAY, "Today we're going to learn how God communicates with us and how we can communicate with Him."

ACTIVITY: COLLECTING DATA

The purpose of this activity is for kids to learn how God communicates with us and to practice communicating with Him.

SUPPLIES PROVIDED BY YOUR ADMINISTRATOR
○ Markers
○ Bibles
○ DATA Letters

INSTRUCTIONS: PART ONE

GATHER kids in a circle and have them pair up with another child.
TELL the kids, "One of the best ways God communicates to us is through the Bible. Let's talk about what God might say to you in two different situations. I'm going to read a situation and give you a

© 2000 Willow Creek Community Church / Small Group Leader's Guidebook

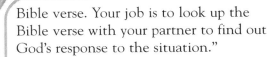

Bible verse. Your job is to look up the Bible verse with your partner to find out God's response to the situation."

Situation 1:
You have a best friend. You have been best friends ever since you were really little. You do absolutely everything together! You share secrets, play games, have sleepovers. But yesterday you found out your friend is moving to a different state! You are really sad. You're not going to have a best friend anymore. You are worried, because you will have no one to give you advice or listen to your secrets. What would God say to you? Read Isaiah 41:10.

SAY, "To look up a Bible verse, start by looking in the front of the Bible at the Table of Contents. Find the book of Isaiah. Turn to that page. Now, there are two kinds of numbers – big numbers and little numbers. The big numbers are chapters. You need chapter 41, so find the big 41. The little numbers are verses. You need verse 10, so when you get to chapter 41, look through it until you get to verse 10."
READ the verse aloud. (*"Do not fear, for I am with you."*)
ASK, "What does this mean?"
(*God would help you no matter what. He is always with you.*)
READ the next situation.

Situation 2:
When you get to school on Friday morning, your teacher reminds the class about the big spelling test you have that afternoon. You hate spelling and you forgot to study. You would have studied if

you had remembered! You're trying to think about the different things you can do. You can just take the test and see what happens, or cheat on the test, or tell the teacher you are sick and need to go to the nurse's office. What would God say to you? Read Colossians 3:9.

SAY, "Now, look up Colossians 3:9 by finding Colossians in the Table of Contents. Then, find the big 3, and the little 9 under that three."
READ the verse out loud. (*Do not lie to each other.*)
ASK, "What does this verse mean?" (*God would want you to tell the truth, not cheat or lie.*)

INSTRUCTIONS: PART TWO
SAY, "We've talked about how reading the Bible is a great way for God to communicate to us, but we can communicate to God, too! In Large Group, you learned one way for us to talk to God. What is it?" (*Prayer*)
TELL the kids, "We can talk to God anytime, anywhere, about anything! An easy way to remember all the things we can pray about is by remembering the word DATA."
PASS OUT a DATA Letter to each kid.
EXPLAIN the following:
"D" stands for "Describe God." We can tell God what we love about Him.
"A" stands for "Ask For Forgiveness." We can tell God when we're sorry for things like lying or not honoring our parents.
"T" stands for "Thank God." We can tell God thanks for anything, like our friends and family.
"A" stands for "Ask." We can ask God to help us or meet our needs.

© 2000 Willow Creek Community Church / Small Group Leader's Guidebook

TELL the kids, "These are four very important parts of a prayer to God. You don't have to say all four in every prayer, but remembering them is a great way to remember all the things you want to say to God."

PUT markers in the middle of your group for kids to use.

SAY, "Now, you have the opportunity to write a letter to God, using the word DATA. You can ask or tell Him anything you would like. You can either write or draw pictures – it is up to you. We will start with the letter 'D'. Does anyone remember what 'D' stands for? That's right, 'Describe God'. Now I'm going to give you a chance to write or draw a picture that describes God."

GATHER ideas from the kids before they begin working, so if a child in your group doesn't have any ideas, the discussion might help them.

CONTINUE working through the other parts of the letter - 'A', 'T', and 'A' in the same way. Ask them what the letter stands for; discuss some ideas and let them draw. When most of the group has finished, move onto the next letter.

WRAP-UP

TELL the kids, "God communicates to us, so we can listen and talk to Him. God wants to talk to us through His Word, the Bible. And not only that, but God wants us to talk to Him, too! God loves it when we pray and talk to Him. He promises to listen when we pray."

BIBLE VERSE

PASS OUT Bible Verse Cards and repeat together. "The Lord will hear when I call to Him." Psalm 4:3

REMIND the kids, "This means God will listen anytime, anyplace, about anything."

PRAYER

Dear God,
Thank You for listening to us. Thank You for letting us pray to You. Thank you for giving us the Bible, so we can hear what You have to say. Amen.

KID CONNECTION CONTINUES. . .

Small Group Leaders, this is a time for you and your group to: continue to build community, let your kids know that you care and pray for them, and better equip you with ways to know how to reach out to each child and/or family.

ASK, "What kinds of things do you wonder about when you think about prayer?"

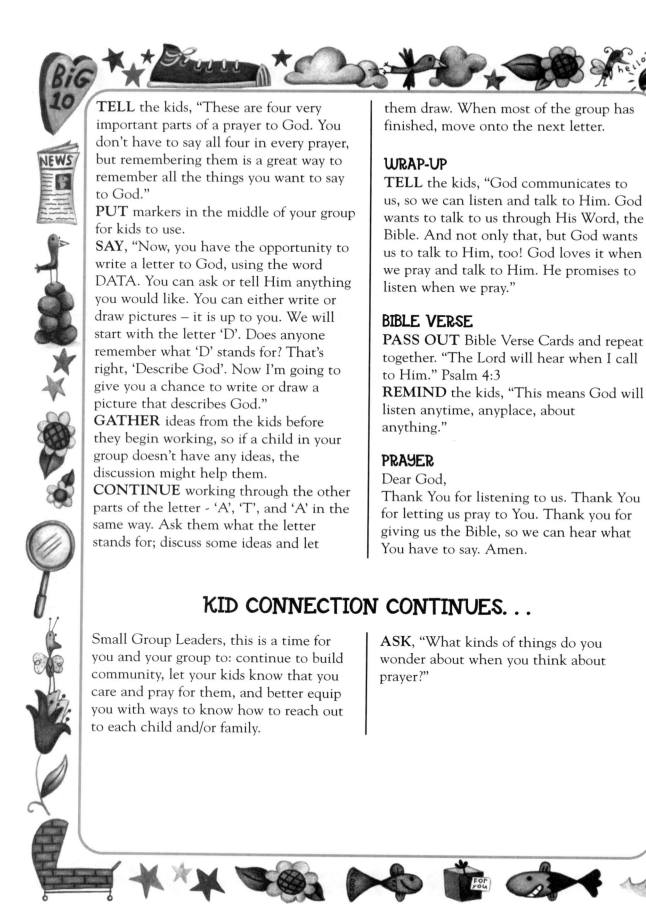

© 2000 Willow Creek Community Church / Small Group Leader's Guidebook

Tell Me A Story
David's Heart

In the beginning when God made the whole earth and everything in it, God also created a beginning to His story. In these upcoming lessons, children will learn the many different eras of God's story within the Old Testament. They will learn about Creation, the first families, and God's promise of salvation. Children will then hear about the Exodus out of Egypt, the Conquests, God's different Kingdoms and the Exile of His people. Our hope within these lessons is to create a sequential view of the Old Testament to make a connection with how people and events fit together, as well as see how we can become part of God's story.

BIBLE STORY
I Samuel 16; I Kings 2:1-4
David was a shepherd boy who was anointed by the priest Samuel to be King of Israel. He had to wait many years to see how God was going to make him a king. He was willing to fight the biggest giant to show his love and devotion to God. Later, he trusted God in the toughest times when King Saul was jealous and tried to kill him. God made him the greatest King in Israel.

BIBLE VERSE
"Man looks at the outward appearance, but the Lord looks at the heart." I Samuel 16:7

KEY CONCEPT
God wants us to love Him with all our hearts.

OBJECTIVES
KNOW WHAT (LG): Children will hear how David was a man who loved, trusted, and followed God.
SO WHAT (LG): Children will learn God wants us to love Him with all our hearts.
NOW WHAT (SG): Children will be challenged to love God with their whole hearts.

SPIRITUAL FORMATION
Loving God

IN ADVANCE DONE BY YOUR ADMINISTRATOR
• Photocopy Bible Verse Cards – one per child (page 39 in Administrator's Guidebook).
• Cut twelve 8" x 8" squares of red felt and twelve 8" x 8" squares of black felt for each Small Group.
• Place the above-mentioned items into a bin for each Small Group Leader.

© 2000 Willow Creek Community Church / Small Group Leader's Guidebook

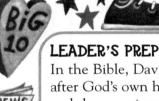

LEADER'S PREP

In the Bible, David is referred to as a man after God's own heart despite his failures and shortcomings. His relationship with Saul is a great example of why he is described this way. Saul was a King who hated David. He made David's life very difficult. He turned people against David and even tried to kill him several times.

Despite these difficulties, David believed God had a plan for his life. He understood that "getting even" was not his job. David knew he was responsible to God for how he responded to difficulty. As you read through I Samuel this week, consider how you respond to difficult people and circumstances. Then, pray that God would help you trust Him with your whole heart.

KID CONNECTION (5 minutes)

WELCOME the kids to Promiseland. Tell them you're glad they're here.
SAY, "Today, we are going to talk about loving God with our whole hearts. Let's talk about what it means to love someone. Tell me about someone you love. How do you show that person that you love him or her?"

TRANSITION
TELL your group, "God wants us to love Him with our whole hearts. Today during Large Group we're going to hear about someone from the Bible who is known for loving God with his whole heart. We just talked about how we show other people we love them. Listen to find out how David showed God he loved Him."

SMALL GROUP (20 minutes)

REVIEW
ASK, "How did David show God he loved Him?" (*He loved God, trusted God, and followed God.*)
REMIND the kids, "David loved God with his whole heart."
ASK the children, "What would you do if you wanted to show God you loved Him with your whole heart?"
TELL the kids, "Today we're going to play a game that will help us see how we can love God with our whole hearts."

ACTIVITY: Heart Skip and Jump
The intention behind Small Group today is for the kids to identify attitudes of the heart.

SUPPLIES PROVIDED BY YOUR ADMINISTRATOR
○ 12 black felt squares
○ 12 red felt squares

SET UP
PLACE the twenty-four felt squares on the floor in four rows of six, so they make a rectangle shape. Put colors in random order. Put squares about two feet apart.

© 2000 Willow Creek Community Church / Small Group Leader's Guidebook

INSTRUCTIONS

TELL the kids, "We're going to play a game called Heart Skip and Jump. I'm going to read a statement. You have to decide whether the statement shows a heart that totally loves God. If it is a statement you would make if you loved God with your whole heart, jump on a red square. If it is a statement that does NOT show a heart that totally loves God, jump on a black square. If you jump on the correctly colored square, you win a point. The person with the most points wins the game. A few HEART STOPPERS are mixed into the statements. When you hear a heart stopper, do what it says. If you succeed, you win a point."

READ the statements.

HAVE the kids keep score of their own points.

SET aside cards that your kids miss to review later.

Answer key:

Y = yes, shows a heart that totally loves God. (Red)

N = no, does not show a heart that totally loves God. (Black)

Heart Skip and Jump Statements

I swear when I stub my toe. N
I make fun of my sister. N
I pray when I'm scared. Y
I asked Jesus to be my forever friend. Y
I want it my way. N
I don't want to share. N
Heart stopper! Do 10 jumping jacks.
God isn't important in my life. N
Who cares what God thinks. N

Heart stopper! Jump on a black square 10 times.
I will share with others. Y
I love my friends. Y
God is the most important thing to me. Y
I want to love others. Y
I use God's name in a bad way. N
I hit my brother when he makes me mad. N
I give God thanks. Y
What I look like is most important. N
Heart stopper! Jog on a red square while repeating the Bible verse of the day.
I want to be first. N
I keep things for myself. N
When I mess up, I tell God I'm sorry. Y
I want it all. N
I want it now. N
I care what God is thinking. Y
Heart stopper! Hop from a red square to a black square 5 times.
I want to obey God. Y
I want to talk to God. Y
I won't do what my parents say. N
I hate my brother. N
I think about what Jesus would do. Y
I want to pray to God. Y
I don't think God can do that. N
I don't care what God says. N
God can do anything. Y
I let others go first. Y
I have to have the coolest clothes. N
People who aren't like me are weird. N
Heart stopper! Switch places with someone close to you.
I go to church. Y
I will defend my sister to others. Y
I tell my friends that I am a Christian. Y
I go along with whatever my friends say. N

© 2000 Willow Creek Community Church / Small Group Leader's Guidebook

WRAP-UP

SIT in a circle on the floor.
GATHER cards kids missed.
TELL the kids, "Let's look at some of the cards you missed. Why do they, or do they not, reflect a heart that loves God? *(various answers)* God is most concerned about our hearts. He wants us to have hearts that love Him, trust Him, and follow Him - just like David did."

BIBLE VERSE

PASS out verse card and repeat together. "Man looks at the outward appearance, but the Lord looks at the heart."
I Samuel 16:7

REMIND the kids, "God doesn't care what you look like. He doesn't judge you based on the brand of shoes you wear or whether you wear glasses. He looks at your heart."

PRAYER

Dear God,
Help us to be more like You. We often have hearts for ourselves, not hearts for You. Thank You for loving us and caring for us. Please help us to have hearts that love You, trust You, and follow You.

KID CONNECTION CONTINUES . . .

Small Group Leaders, this is a time for you and your group to: continue to build community, let your kids know that you care about them as individuals, hear their felt needs, and to better equip you in knowing how to specifically pray or reach out to each child.

ASK, "When is it hard to show you have a heart that loves God? When is it easy to show you have a heart that loves God?"

© 2000 Willow Creek Community Church / Small Group Leader's Guidebook

Tell Me a Story
Elijah and Baal

In the beginning when God made the whole earth and everything in it, God also created a beginning to His story. In these upcoming lessons, children will learn the many different eras of God's story within the Old Testament. They will learn about Creation, the first families, and God's promise of salvation. Children will then hear about the Exodus out of Egypt, the Conquests, God's different Kingdoms and the Exile of His people. Our hope within these lessons is to create a sequential view of the Old Testament to make a connection with how people and events fit together, as well as see how we can become part of God's story.

BIBLE STORY
I Kings 18:16-39
God showed Himself to be the one true God. King Ahab and his people worshiped false gods. The prophet Elijah challenged King Ahab to a contest. They were each to make a sacrifice to their god. Whichever god answered by igniting the altar with fire was the true god. Ahab called out to Baal, and Baal did not answer. When nothing happened, Elijah called out to God. God showed His power by igniting the water-drenched altar. When the people saw this, they bowed down to worship God.

BIBLE VERSE
"You shall have no other gods before me."
Exodus 20:3

KEY CONCEPT
God is the One True God and I can choose to follow only Him.

OBJECTIVES
KNOW WHAT (LG): Children will hear the story of how God showed Himself as the One True God when Elijah and the prophets of Baal had a contest on Mount Carmel.
SO WHAT (LG): Children will learn that God is the only true God.
NOW WHAT (SG): Children will identify ways they can choose to follow God.

SPIRITUAL FORMATION
Obedience

IN ADVANCE DONE BY YOUR ADMINISTRATOR
- Photocopy My Story Sheets – one per child (*page 41 in Administrator's Guidebook*).
- Photocopy Bible Verse Cards and cut apart – one per child (*page 40 in Administrator's Guidebook*).
- Gather markers. Each group needs a variety of colors.
- Place the above-mentioned items in a bin for each Small Group leader.

© 2000 Willow Creek Community Church / Small Group Leader's Guidebook

LEADER'S PREP

The prophet Elijah had tremendous courage and faith. He had an ability to trust God in a way that allowed him to challenge those who didn't believe what he knew to be true -- that the Lord is the One True God. As you read through I Kings this week, consider the people in your life who don't believe as you do about God. Maybe it's at work, or maybe it's with your friends and family – but consider what steps of faith you can take that might help those people worship the One True God.

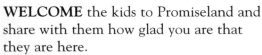

KID CONNECTION (5 minutes)

WELCOME the kids to Promiseland and share with them how glad you are that they are here.
ASK, "Who are your favorite heroes? Who are your favorite superheros? Why?"
ASK, "What kinds of cool things can these superheros do?"
ASK, "Would you follow these heroes? Why or why not?"

TRANSITION

TELL your group, "Today in Large Group, we are going to hear a story about a man who chose to only follow the One True God. Listen and try to find out what he did to follow God."

SMALL GROUP (20 minutes)

REVIEW

TELL the kids, "In Large Group today we learned that God is the One True God."
ASK, "What did Elijah do to follow God as the One True God?" (*He didn't worship Baal, he prayed only to God and no one else.*)
SAY, "God is the only one who knows everything and has all the answers – He is the only one who has the power to change our lives. God is the One True God and we can choose to follow only Him like Elijah."
TELL the children, "Today we're going to do an activity that will encourage us to follow God."

ACTIVITY: MY STORY

The intention behind Small Group is for the kids to think of and draw a story about a time when they followed God. They will encourage one another to continue to follow God by sharing their stories.

SUPPLIES PROVIDED BY YOUR ADMINISTRATOR
○ Markers
○ My Story Sheets

INSTRUCTIONS: Part 1

TELL the kids, "This is not an art contest!"
SHARE a story about a time when you chose to follow God. Share an

Page 56

appropriate story, maybe a time when you were a child.

SAY, "Today in Large Group time, we talked about following God. When we follow God, we follow His commands. Think of a time in life when you followed God and His commands." (*When you obeyed your parents or teacher, when a friend asked you to do something you knew was wrong, when you didn't lie or cheat, or when you were kind to someone when everyone else was being mean.*)

GIVE kids one minute or so to think of an example.

PASS out the My Story Sheets.

INSTRUCTIONS: Part 2

SHARE stories one at a time.

ASK after each child shares, "How did (*child's name*) follow God in his/her story?"

REPEAT for each child who shares his or her My Story sheet.

TELL the kids, "Our God is the One True God. He is the only God. He wants us to only follow Him. Nothing else and no one else is worth following! **GOD IS THE ONE TRUE GOD AND YOU CAN CHOOSE TO FOLLOW ONLY HIM."**

WRAP-UP

TELL the kids, "You're going to take ten minutes and draw a comic strip of your story about a time when you chose to follow God. In the first box, draw the situation. In the second box, draw what happened in your story. In the third box, draw the outcome of your decision to follow God. When you are done drawing, you will be able to share them with the group."

BIBLE VERSE

PASS out verse card and repeat together. "You shall have no other gods before me." Exodus 20:3

REMIND the kids, "We are to follow God, and follow nothing before Him. When we follow His commands, we follow Him."

PRAYER

Dear God,
Thank You for being the One True God. We love You. Please help us to follow You first. Help us to put You first in our lives. Amen.

KID CONNECTION CONTINUES . . .

Small Group Leaders, this is your time for you and your group to: continue to build community, let your kids know that you care about them as individuals, hear their felt needs, and to better equip you in

knowing how to specifically pray or reach out to each kid.

ASK, "What is your favorite _____?" (*Color, game, food, sport . . .*)

© 2000 Willow Creek Community Church / Small Group Leader's Guidebook

Tell Me a Story
Jonah

In the beginning when God made the whole earth and everything in it, God also created a beginning to His story. In these upcoming lessons, children will learn the many different eras of God's story within the Old Testament. They will learn about Creation, the first families, and God's promise of salvation. Children will then hear about the Exodus out of Egypt, the Conquests, God's different Kingdoms and the Exile of His people. Our hope within these lessons is to create a sequential view of the Old Testament to make a connection with how people and events fit together, as well as see how we can become part of God's story.

BIBLE STORY

Jonah 1–3

God told Jonah to go to Nineveh, but Jonah ran from God and began traveling to Tarshish on a ship. The Lord caused a great storm because of Jonah's disobedience and Jonah was thrown overboard. A big fish swallowed Jonah, and Jonah remained in the fish for three days. After confessing his sin and asking God to forgive him, God forgave Jonah and gave him another chance to go to Nineveh and deliver God's message. The Ninevites confessed their sin and God forgave them.

BIBLE VERSE

"If we confess our sins He is faithful and just and will forgive us our sins." I John 1:9

KEY CONCEPT
God is forgiving and I can go to Him every time I sin and ask for forgiveness.

OBJECTIVES

KNOW WHAT (LG): Children will hear the story of Jonah running from God. After turning back to God, God forgave him and gave him another chance to go to Nineveh and deliver God's message.
SO WHAT (LG): Children will learn that God is forgiving and wants us to go to Him every time we sin.
NOW WHAT (SG): Children will identify times that they can go to God and ask for forgiveness.

SPIRITUAL FORMATION

Confession

IN ADVANCE DONE BY YOUR ADMINISTRATOR

- Photocopy Sin Cards and cut apart – one set of eight per group (*page 43-44 in Administrator's Guidebook*).
- Photocopy Bible Verse Cards and cut apart – one per child (*page 42 in Administrator's Guidebook*).
- Gather plain pieces of paper and markers – one per child.
- Place aforementioned items in a bin for each Small Group leader.

© 2000 Willow Creek Community Church / Small Group Leader's Guidebook

LEADER'S PREP

Sometimes we get busy with life and we don't hear God speak. Other times we hear God speak and choose not to follow Him, like Jonah. Our goal should be to hear God and then follow what He says, but that doesn't always happen. So like Jonah, when we sin and disobey, we can do a mid-course turn-around and ask for forgiveness. This week as you read through Jonah 1-3 think about whether you might need to make a mid-course turn-around. Ask the Holy Spirit to help you become aware of areas where you are not following God, so you can change course right now.

KID CONNECTION (5 minutes)

WELCOME the kids to Promiseland and tell them you are glad they are here.
ASK, "Who are some of the people in your life you need to obey? (*parents, teachers, coaches, babysitters*) What are some consequences of being disobedient?" (*Talk about natural consequences, such as getting hurt if you climb a tree you aren't supposed to, versus imposed consequences, such as losing privileges or getting grounded.*)

TRANSITION

TELL your group, "Today in Large Group we are going to hear a story about a man who disobeyed God, even after God told him specifically what he needed to do. There were some crazy consequences for his disobedience. In Large Group, find out what happened to him when he disobeyed God."

SMALL GROUP (20 minutes)

REVIEW

ASK the kids, "What happened when Jonah disobeyed God? (*There was a huge storm, and then he was swallowed by a big fish.*) What did Jonah do while he was in the big fish?" (*He confessed his sins to God and asked for forgiveness.*)
SAY, "Jonah knew he had sinned when he disobeyed God. When he was in the fish he learned God is forgiving and he could go to Him and ask for forgiveness. When we sin, we can ask for forgiveness, too. We're going to play a game to help us recognize when we can go to God and ask for forgiveness."

ASKING FOR FORGIVENESS ACTIVITY

The intention behind this Small Group activity is for the kids to think of and identify times when they have sinned, and to learn they can go to God and ask for forgiveness when they sin.

SUPPLIES PROVIDED BY YOUR ADMINISTRATOR
○ Plain Paper
○ Markers
○ Sin Cards
○ Paper bags

© 2000 Willow Creek Community Church / Small Group Leader's Guidebook

SET UP

DIVIDE the group into pairs.
GIVE each pair one of the Sin Cards and a marker.

INSTRUCTIONS: PART 1

TELL the kids, "Talk with your partner, and then write down on your Sin Card why you think people do the sin on your card. For example, people lie sometimes because they are afraid they will get into trouble if they tell the truth."
GIVE them a five minutes to write things down.
SHARE each team's answers with the whole group.

INSTRUCTIONS: PART 2

COLLECT the Sin Cards.
PASS out a sheet of plain paper and a marker to each kid.
TELL the kids, "A few weeks ago we learned that everybody sins. God tells us all have sinned. Now, I'm going to put a Sin Card in the center of the group. Then, I'm going to read a question about that sin. If you can think of a time when you sinned in this way, draw an X on your piece of paper. No talking while I'm asking questions – just listen. Think about the question and draw on your papers."
DO this exercise yourself, along with the kids.
READ the following questions:
Have you ever lied? If so, draw an X on the paper. *(Give kids a few seconds to think.)*
Have you ever stolen something? If so, draw an X on your paper. *(Give kids a few seconds to think.)*
Have you ever loved something more than you love God? If so, draw an X on

the paper. *(Give kids a few seconds to think.)*
Have you ever disobeyed your parents? If so, draw an X on the paper. *(Give kids a few seconds to think.)*
Have you ever made fun of someone? If so, draw an X on the paper. *(Give kids a few seconds to think.)*
Have you ever disobeyed a teacher? If so, draw an X on the paper. *(Give kids a few seconds to think.)*
Have you ever hit or kicked someone when you were mad or frustrated? If so, draw an X on the paper. *(Give kids a few seconds to think.)*
Have you ever cheated on something? If so, draw an X on the paper. *(Give kids a few seconds to think.)*

INSTRUCTIONS: PART 3

TELL the kids, "God is forgiving. He will forgive us no matter what! God wants us to go to Him each and every time we sin and ask Him for forgiveness. What do you think we should do about the sins on the pieces of paper we have? *(Pray and ask for forgiveness.)* Let's ask forgiveness right now for these things that we wrote down. I'm going to give you some time to silently confess your sins to God if you so choose. Then, after a couple minutes, I will jump in and close in prayer."
PRAY silently. After a few minutes, pray aloud, confessing and asking forgiveness for the sins on your sheets of paper.
PUT the paper bag in the middle of your group.
SAY, "If you prayed to confess your sins, God has forgiven you! In His eyes, those sins are gone. Crumple up your paper and throw it in this paper bag! Then, I'm going to throw them in the garbage."

© 2000 Willow Creek Community Church / Small Group Leader's Guidebook

WRAP-UP

TELL the kids, "We saw that Jonah wanted to do his own thing and go his own way. He would have been much better off if he had obeyed God in the beginning! We do things like that in our lives, too. We go our own way, trying to ignore God. When we mess up, we can turn-around, like we did in the Large Group Turn-Around Game, and ask God to forgive us. No matter what you've done, God is forgiving and you can go to Him every time you sin and ask for forgiveness."

BIBLE VERSE

PASS out verse card and repeat together. "If we confess our sins, He is faithful and just and will forgive us our sins." I John 1:9
REMIND the kids, "This verse means God will always forgive us when we tell Him we are sorry for our sins."

PRAYER

Dear God,
Thank You for forgiving us when we sin. Help us to follow You. When we don't follow You, help us to remember we can always come to You and ask for forgiveness. Amen.

KID CONNECTION CONTINUES . . .

Small Group Leaders, this is your time for you and your group to: continue to build community, let your kids know that you care about them as individuals, hear their felt needs, and to better equip you in

knowing how to specifically pray or reach out to each kid.

ASK, "What are some things that you are thankful for this Thanksgiving?"

© 2000 Willow Creek Community Church / Small Group Leader's Guidebook

Tell Me a Story
Shadrach, Meshach, and Abednego

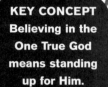

In the beginning when God made the whole earth and everything in it, God also created a beginning to His story. In these upcoming lessons, children will learn the many different eras of God's story within the Old Testament. They will learn about Creation, the first families, and God's promise of salvation. Children will then hear about the Exodus out of Egypt, the Conquests, God's different Kingdoms and the Exile of His people. Our hope within these lessons is to create a sequential view of the Old Testament to make a connection with how people and events fit together, as well as see how we can become part of God's story.

BIBLE STORY

Daniel 3:1-30

In today's lesson, children will hear the story of Shadrach, Meshach, and Abednego. When King Nebuchadnezzar reigned, he made a huge idol of gold to be worshiped in his kingdom. Shadrach, Meshach, and Abednego stood up to the king and told him they would not worship a false god. Because of this, King Nebuchadnezzar had them thrown into a hot, fiery furnace. To the king's amazement, they walked around inside the furnace without being burned or harmed at all. They were protected by the Almighty God. In the end, the king praised and worshiped God, because he knew God protected His followers.

BIBLE VERSE

"Be strong in the Lord and in His mighty power."
Ephesians 6:10

KEY CONCEPT
Believing in the One True God means standing up for Him.

OBJECTIVES

KNOW WHAT: (LG) Children will hear the story of Shadrach, Meshach, and Abednego and how they stood up for God by not worshipping idols even if it meant they might die in a furnace.
SO WHAT: (LG) Children will learn believing in the One True God means standing up for Him.
NOW WHAT: (SG) Children will be challenged to think of ways they can stand up for God in their lives.

SPIRITUAL FORMATION

Commitment/Courage

IN ADVANCE DONE BY YOUR ADMINISTRATOR

- Photocopy Bible Verse Cards and cut apart – one per child (*page 45 in Administrator's Guidebook*).
- Photocopy Match Me Game Cards – one set per Small Group (*pages 46-48 in Administrator's Guidebook*).
- Place above-mentioned items in a bin for each Small Group leader.

© 2000 Willow Creek Community Church / Small Group Leader's Guidebook

LEADER'S PREP

Read Daniel 3. Shadrach, Meshach, and Abednego are worthy of our respect. They stood up for God in a way that most people will never have to face. They had every reason to believe they were going to die, but God chose to perform a miracle for all the people to see. While most of us have religious freedom, some people in the world today are being persecuted for being Christians. You may not have to choose Christ or death, but you do have the opportunity to stand up for God in smaller ways. Maybe you could tell a co-worker about God, or talk candidly when a friend asks you about church. Whatever it may be, meet the challenge to stand up for God and what you believe. This week, think about the ways you might stand up for God. Pray for the opportunity to declare what you believe.

KID CONNECTION (5 minutes)

WELCOME the kids to Promiseland and tell them you are glad they are here.
SHARE a story about a time when you were able to stand up for what you believe in.
ASK, "What are some times you feel pressure to follow other people instead of standing up for God?" (home, school, sports)

TRANSITION

TELL your group, "Today in Large Group we are going to hear a story about three men who felt pressure to worship something other than God. Instead of doing what was easy, they stood up for God and what they believed. Watch carefully to see HOW they stood up for God."

SMALL GROUP (20 minutes)

REVIEW

ASK the kids, "How did Shadrach, Meshach, and Abednego stand up for God – What did they do?" (They told the king that they would not worship his gold idol.)
SAY, "We learned from the story today that **BELIEVING IN THE ONE TRUE GOD MEANS STANDING UP FOR HIM.** That was important for Shadrach, Meshach, and Abednego, and it is important for us. Today, we are going to think about ways to stand up for God in our own lives.

ACTIVITY: THE MATCH ME GAME

The intention behind Small Group today is for the kids to think about ways that they can stand up for God in their lives.

SUPPLIES PROVIDED BY YOUR ADMINISTRATOR

Match Me Game Cards – one set

SET UP

HAVE kids sit in a circle on the floor.
SPREAD OUT Match Me Game Cards face down on the floor in a 6x4 rectangle.

© 2000 Willow Creek Community Church / Small Group Leader's Guidebook

INSTRUCTIONS

TELL the kids, "We're going to play the Match Me Game. It is like many other memory games you may have played. I have put twenty-four cards face down on the floor. When it is your turn, choose two cards to turn over and look at – everyone gets to see them. Each card has a match somewhere on the floor. The goal of the game is to collect as many matching cards as you can. Whoever has the most matches at the end of the game wins.

SAY, "There is a catch! When you find two matching cards, in order to collect them you must make up an example of how to stand up for God in that particular place or situation. It can be made up, or you can use a real-life example. If you can't think of an example, you may ask one other person for help. There are two sets of 'You Choose' cards in the deck. You can make up any situation if you choose these cards."

TAKE turns around the circle.

REPEAT the game as much as time allows.

MATCH ME GAME CARDS

School	Radio
Friends	Playing Sports
Home	Church
Movie Theater	Park
Family	TV

WRAP-UP

TELL the kids, "Believing in the One True God means standing up for Him. You gave some good examples of ways you could stand up for God. Remember those this week! Sometimes it's really hard for us to stand up and have the courage to do things God's way. But like our Bible Verse says, we can be strong, and be bold, because we know God has all the power."

BIBLE VERSE

PASS out Bible Verse cards and repeat verse together. "Be strong in the Lord and in His mighty power." Ephesians 6:10

REMIND the kids, "This verse means that God will help you when you stand up for Him. He will be with you, just like He was with Shadrach, Meshach, and Abednego."

PRAYER

Dear God,
We believe in You. We believe You are the One True God. Please help us to stand up for You. Amen.

KID CONNECTION CONTINUES . . .

Small Group leaders, this is your time for you and your group to: continue to build community, let your kids know that you care about them as individuals, hear their felt needs, and to better equip you in knowing how to specifically pray or reach out to each child.

ASK, "What are some things that you love to do after school?"

© 2000 Willow Creek Community Church / Small Group Leader's Guidebook